# Sandwriter

# Sandwriter

## MONICA HUGHES

Henry Holt and Company · New York

First published in the United States in 1988 by
Henry Holt and Company, Inc., 115 West 18th Street,
New York, New York 10011.

Library of Congress Cataloging-in-Publication Data
Hughes, Monica.
Sandwriter.
Summary: Traveling to the desert island of Roshan
to meet the young man that her aunt wants her to marry,
Princess Antia becomes involved in a deadly power
struggle when she uncovers secrets surrounding the
ancient mystery of Roshan and the identity of the
Sandwriter.
[1. Fantasy]  I. Title.
PZ7.H87364San  1988     [Fic]      87-21198
ISBN 0-8050-0617-6

First American Edition
Printed in the United States of America
10  9  8  7  6  5  4  3  2  1

ISBN 0-8050-0617-6

# Sandwriter

# 1

Antia swung idly to and fro under the shade of the big *chepa* tree. Her silver gauze dress fluttered in the breeze made by her swinging. To and fro. To and fro . . .

I'm so bored, she thought. Bored, bored! She slid from the swing and ran across the grass toward the shaded seat where Nan sat. "Nan, what are you doing?"

"Nothing, Highness, nothing." Nan's gnarled hands guiltily covered the box in her lap.

"Nan, you liar! Let me see." She snatched the small carved box and held it tantalizingly just beyond Nan's reach. "Now what's in here? Why, zaramint candies! And the box half empty, too."

"Give them back, pet. Don't tease."

"They're bad for you. You're too fat already." Antia took a candy from the box and bit it neatly in two. Then, suddenly bored with teasing her nurse, she tossed the box back into the old woman's lap and began to pace up and down the walled garden.

"Princess, it's too hot. You will make yourself sick. Come and sit in the shade."

Antia ignored the anxious voice. "I am bored . . . bored . . . bored." The sound of the word fitted perfectly the secluded

1

garden, the carved stone of the palace walls, the pitiless blue sky and the interminable heat. *Bored*.

She went swiftly up the steps and through the archway into the palace. Inside all was dark and cool. Fans whispered under the vaulted ceiling that ran the full length of the building to the main entrance, where another arch mirrored the one through which she had just come. Beyond it lay the glaring white of midday.

Servants moved softly here and there, their embroidered slippers flapping against the tiled floor. On the carved benches and on the floor outside the audience room, suppliants waited patiently.

Antia sighed. It would have been pleasant to talk to Uncle Rangor, or to try and beat him in a game of castles, but he seemed nowadays to be always busy. She did not scratch on the carved door of the Queen's apartment to ask admittance. In fact, she ran past it on tiptoe. Aunt Sankath would have no sympathy with her feelings, but would scold and set her to doing endless embroidery.

Under the arch of the main entrance the heat and light struck at one like a blow. For a moment Antia was blinded and stopped, steadying herself against one of the stone pillars of the wide veranda, until her eyes adjusted. Formal trees surrounded the circular driveway, which was of white sand brushed ten times a day by one of the gardeners, and her view of the main gate and the enticing world that lay beyond was hidden by a great fountain.

Against the left side of the main door a soldier leaned. She watched his eyelids droop, open again, close, and she swallowed a giggle. A quick look around. Nobody else in sight.

In a whirl of silver draperies she ran down the steps and around the fountain to the left, where a venerable *thoka* tree spread its branches invitingly. She tucked up her skirt and began to climb, staying as much as possible on the side away from the palace, the side away from prying eyes.

There! Her favorite branch, smooth barked, canopied by the wide many-fingered leaves of the branch above. She lay along it on her stomach and peered cautiously through the leaves. Past the curve of silver water she could see the head and shoulders of the sentry. He had overcome his sleepiness and was walking briskly to and fro. Time for his relief and he doesn't want to be caught dozing, she thought.

She turned away and looked over to the left, to the world outside the palace wall. It was so very interesting out there. A cart creaked by, piled high with brightly colored fruit and vegetables and pulled by an ancient and dusty lema. Beside it walked a girl, no more than fifteen or sixteen years old – *my* age, thought Antia enviously. Her feet and legs were bare and her black hair hung loosely down her back. She was wearing a cotton dress as bright as the fruit, wide-skirted and short, with a blouse that showed her arms. They, as well as her face and legs, were tanned, and she walked with a spring, singing to herself and slapping the flank of the lema encouragingly.

Antia sighed and watched the girl out of sight. Then she looked at herself. Her silver dress reached to her ankles and her long black hair had been twisted by Nan into a bun on top of her head and covered with a silver net embroidered with pearls. Like a dressed-up doll, she thought.

What would it be like to be free? Suppose she were to slip out of the gate while the sentry's back was turned and follow that cart down the road, maybe make friends with the girl? I wonder where she's going? To market, I suppose. She hesitated, weighing the risks. But she was bound to be noticed and some gossiping servant would tell the Queen. Then she would be beaten and shut in her room for days. It wasn't worth it. She sighed again.

If only Eskoril would come and take me riding. I'm never

bored when Eskoril is here. At dawn was the best time, out into the wooded countryside around Malan. He used to call at her window and she would wake at his voice, scramble into her riding habit, and tiptoe out to join him, leaving Nan snoring.

But now Eskoril was away from the palace on some state business and, oh, how she missed him. No, not him. That was stupid. After all, he was only her tutor and at least thirty years old. It wasn't *he* that she missed, just the riding, and the lessons that he made so interesting: mathematics and astronomy and statecraft. That was why she was bored and depressed. She was missing the riding and her lessons, that was all.

Her thoughts were interrupted by the sound of cheering and the clip-clop of hoofs. She leaned perilously far out of her tree. A covered carriage appeared, drawn by four dappled browns. The King's number one carriage, with his pennant flying. No, not his. As the carriage turned in at the gate and passed directly beneath her, she could see that the pennant was Roshan's. Roshan? The island desert across the Small Sea. Who could possibly be visiting them from Roshan?

The carriage stopped below the main steps and servants appeared out of the shadows to line the entrance. Then a man stepped down from the carriage and held out his arm to someone within. Her heart skipped. Why, it was Eskoril! And who was he escorting? She nearly fell from her branch in her effort to see.

A woman, swathed in white, for all the world, Antia thought with a giggle, as if she were dressed in bed sheets. The hand resting on Eskoril's arm was brown, as brown as that of a common peasant. No rings, no bracelets. Antia glanced complacently at the jewels on her own white hands and arms.

The stranger mounted the steps with Eskoril and turned at the top to glance around the courtyard. Her eyes stopped at the thoka tree and looked straight into Antia's. They were small eyes, as dark as a bird's, and her nose was long and straight, her lips firm. Someone to be reckoned with, Antia thought, ducking back under the leaves. But who can she be? And why have I heard nothing of this visit before?

Uncle Rangor and Aunt Sankath appeared and there were greetings and embraces, as if between equals. After that was over everyone went into the darkness of the palace, Eskoril limping behind them. She was tempted to call out to him, but decided against it. Aunt Sankath had the eyes of a hawk and the ears of a bat.

She waited impatiently until the matched dapple browns had drawn the carriage around to the stables, and the sentry had once more slumped against the archway. Then she climbed down the tree, only tearing her gauze a very little on a protruding twig. She slipped into the palace, ran across the great hall, and out into the walled garden at the back.

"Nan, Nan! Drat the woman! Where is she? Nan!"

Her nurse had not moved from her seat under the chepa tree. Her hands were folded over the candy box in her lap. Her eyes were closed and she snored faintly. Antia ran across the grass and pulled at her sleeve.

"Nan, Nan, do wake up! A woman has arrived from Roshan. Someone important, I think."

"Huh? What's that, my pet? What is important?"

"This woman from Roshan. And, oh, Nan, Eskoril is back, and now I won't be bored anymore. There'll be lessons and riding and . . ."

"Humph!" Nan sat up and shook herself. For some reason she had never liked Eskoril, though he was the handsomest, cleverest, kindest man in the world.

"Don't 'humph' at me, Nan. Tell me about this woman. You hear all the palace gossip. You must know who she is."

5

"I know nothing, Princess. Nothing. I'm only your old nanny and nobody ever tells me anything."

"What nonsense! You're a sly old woman and you see everything that's happening in the palace and hear twice as much as that. Tell me, clever, dear Nan."

"Don't tease, naughty one. You'll hear all about it from Her Majesty, I'm sure. All in good time."

"What's Aunt Sankath to do with this visit? Oh, tell me, come on, do."

"I mustn't. Don't tease me, pet. You'll get me all in a lather and it's too hot for that. I swear every summer gets hotter." She fanned herself with her handkerchief.

"You're getting fatter, Nan, that's the trouble. Look, you've eaten the whole boxful. Oh, Nan, you are ... "

"Antia!" The cold voice was quiet, but it cut through the teasing and the hot lazy afternoon and the heady smell of ripening chepas like a sword.

Antia jumped to her feet and curtsied. "Yes, Aunt Sankath."

The Queen stood in the shadow of the carved archway, her hand resting on the stone sea serpents that writhed up the pillar. She wore her second best official gown, and her smooth black hair was adorned with a coronet of precious stones.

"You are to meet our guest. Come here and let me see you. Tcha! Dust and filth! And a tear in your hem. How do you manage to get into such a state? Your nurse gives you far too much freedom. Well, we'll talk about *that* later. Go and change at once. You must bathe, you're as dirty as your dress. Then put on your ... let me see ... yes, your blue gauze with the silver embroidery and the cap with sapphires. See to it, Nurse." She swept back into the palace without waiting for an answer, as Nan scrambled to her feet and bobbed a curtsey.

"There now. You see what happens when you run around

6

like a rough boy? *I* get into trouble, that's what. No use my telling her you never heed me, is there? She'll only have me thrown out to starve in my old age."

"You'll never starve, you silly old thing, I promise. And *she* can't dismiss you. You're my very own Nan and you've been mine for sixteen years and she shan't touch you."

"Bless you, my pet, but you don't know what she's capable of, if she makes up her mind to it. Come, hurry now. We mustn't keep her waiting or bad will become worse." She bustled into the palace, calling for servants.

Twenty minutes later, bathed in scented water, dressed in her best blue gown, with her hair so tightly confined within the cap of silver and sapphires that her eyebrows were pulled up into a surprised arch, Antia approached the door of the council chamber. A servant sprang to open it and she swept in, her chin high though her heart thumped with curiosity, and waited politely inside the door.

The King and Queen were sitting at a low table placed near the window, through which a small breeze now drifted. Between them sat the stranger, her head bare to show soft wavy brown hair.

"Come here. Don't just stand there like an awkward schoolgirl."

Antia sighed inwardly. If she *had* come right up to the table Aunt Sankath would have accused her of being forward. There was no pleasing her. She crossed the room, curtsied to her uncle and aunt, and then, after an instant's hesitation, to the stranger. The birdlike eyes sparkled with hidden laughter. It was hard not to smile back.

The King took her hand. "Lady Sofi, this is our niece, Antia, the only child of our dear younger brother . . ."

"Yes, indeed. Were not her parents killed in an . . . ?"

"It was a hunting accident," the Queen snapped, a spot of color bright in each cheek.

7

"Of course, I remember. Dear child, come here."

Antia held out her hand which was taken, patted, and then held. "But I have seen you before, have I not?" The eyes twinkled.

Antia bit her lip. So she had been spotted up in the tree! If the Lady Sofi gave her away she'd be on bread and water for a week. "I don't believe we have ever *met*, Lady Sofi," she said quickly.

"Perhaps you are right. My eyes are not as keen as they once were. My husband teases me that in Roshan, where everyone can see like the desert hawk, I can only see across a room." Lady Sofi released her hand with a gentle squeeze and turned to the Queen. "She is charming. You must be very proud of her. Now tell me, what does she think of our plan?"

"She is only a child. I do not discuss matters of state with children," Queen Sankath snapped. "She will do as she is told."

"Forgive me." The Lady Sofi's voice was gentle but firm. "I will not permit the plan to be carried out without the Princess's understanding and cooperation. Anything else would be abominable."

The Queen's mouth puckered as if she had bitten into an unripe chepa. "In good time. It is enough for the Princess to know that Lady Sofi wishes to take her back to Roshan with her."

Antia felt as if she had been pushed off a cliff. "For a visit?" she managed to stammer.

"For a long visit."

"But why? Oh, Aunt Sankath, what have I done wrong? Why must I go to Roshan? It is all desert and dirt and flies."

"You forget yourself. And you insult our guest." The Queen's voice was icy.

"I . . . I'm sorry, Lady Sofi. I forgot. Ma'am, I don't even know who you are."

8

The eyes twinkled understandingly. "I am the wife of Chief Hamrab, who is the ruler of Roshan. And truly, our country is not all desert. And definitely not all dirt and flies! I do hope you will come and stay with us."

"But why? I mean . . . thank you very much, ma'am. But why are you honoring me with this invitation?"

Lady Sofi glanced at the Queen, and Antia saw Aunt Sankath frown and shake her head. "I would like to get to know you better, my dear. As for the rest . . . well, perhaps it is wiser to wait before we talk of it. Think about it. Perhaps we can talk again after dinner."

Obeying the jerk of Aunt Sankath's head Antia curtseyed and left the room. She ran across the great hall to her own apartment. "Oh, Nan, guess what. That woman is the wife of Chief Hamrab. She's asked me to go back with her to Roshan, not just for a ten-day or so, but for ages. Imagine it! What an idea! I won't go and that's the end of it."

"The Queen'll make you go if that's what she wants."

"No, she won't. Lady Sofi – she's nice, not a bit what I expected a Roshanite to be like, I thought they were all dirty and ignorant – anyway, she says I shan't have to go unless I choose to. So there!"

"Her Majesty has her ways. You'll go and I'll be out of work, you'll see." She sniffed.

"You'll stay with me forever, I swear." Antia knelt beside her chair. "And when you're too old to take care of me I shall take care of you."

"There, my dove, don't get in a snit. Perhaps you're right. Perhaps you won't have to go." She sniffed again and a tear ran down her cheek. "Oh dear."

"What is it? There's more to it than just a visit, isn't there? Something you're not telling me."

"She'd have my tongue if I told you."

"Statecraft. Between Kamalant and Roshan." Antia walked

9

up and down the gauze-draped room. "A matter of state." She turned and stared at her nurse. "Why, Aunt Sankath is planning to marry me off, isn't she? No, you don't have to say anything. I can tell by your face. Well, I won't and that's the end of it. The sneaky thing!"

"I didn't say a word to you, mind. Not a hint."

"Of course you didn't, Nan. Well, if I refuse to go to Roshan I won't have to meet this stupid person Aunt Sankath wants me to marry. So I just won't go. It's as simple as that!"

A ten-day later Antia stood in the stern of the royal barque of Roshan, watching the forests and mountains of Kamalant dwindle and vanish into a clouded horizon. Beside her Nan lamented loudly. " . . . that I should live to see this day, never to set foot in my dear Kamalant again . . . "

"Hush, Nan, they'll hear you." Antia glanced at the bronzed crewmen, busily tightening and coiling ropes on the deck nearby.

"Much I care. Ignorant lot!" Nan sniffed but lowered her voice. "I mean, just look at this ship. Sail! It'll take us three ten-days to reach Lohat. Royal barque indeed! Why couldn't we have come all comfortable like on one of His Majesty's new steamships?"

Antia laughed. "You'd have been even more frightened in one of those noisy things than aboard this ship. What a fraud you are, Nan!"

"Pot calling kettle sooty, miss! Who wasn't going to go to Roshan whatever happened?"

Antia blushed. "That . . . that's quite different. Eskoril explained to me how necessary it was for me to go. For . . . for matters of state. *You* wouldn't understand," she added loftily. The rest was a secret between her and Eskoril and she would never breathe a word to Nan, no matter how much her old nurse teased her.

10

But she thought a great deal about her fateful meeting with Eskoril during the long days when the royal barque wallowed across the sea that separated the twin continents of Kamalant and Komilant from the great island of Roshan. During the nights too, as she lay in a cramped wooden bed in a small stuffy cabin with Nan snoring loudly beside her.

Eskoril had picked a moment when Nan was dozing beneath her favorite tree to slip out of the palace into the garden, like a shadow from among the shadows. Antia had looked up from the swing where she had been idly sitting, tracing patterns on the gravel with her toe, to see him beckon silently. Then he had limped quickly away into the rose garden to the south. She had jumped from the swing and followed him, her embroidered slippers making no noise on the white gravel paths.

Her heart was pounding as she came close. He had hardly said a word to her since he had come back, not a word, and yet they had been such friends before. She felt uneasily that he must be angry with her, but she did not know why. Proudly she decided that she would pretend that nothing was different.

"How mysterious you are!" she exclaimed gaily. He was bending over a particularly fine bloom, inspecting it as if he were getting it by heart. He put a finger to his lips, but his eyes did not meet hers. Oh, Eskoril, how I do love you, she thought desperately. What is wrong? What have I done?

She filled the silence between them with whispered chatter. "We haven't been riding for I don't know how many ten-days, and as for my studies, I am sorely behind without your guidance. What has kept you away from the palace for so long?"

"Affairs of state."

That stupid phrase again. Everything these days was affairs of state, from Aunt Sankath's rages to the crazy idea that she

11

should be sent to live in Roshan. She kicked at the white stones on the path. "Pick me a rose, Eskoril," she ordered. "That one, since it seems so special."

He ignored her request, but looked up suddenly, pinning her with his piercing black eyes. She stared back. They were strange eyes, seeming to have little or no iris. They looked like dark bottomless pools, dangerous but attractive.

"Why did you not accept the Lady Sofi's invitation to Roshan?" he asked abruptly. Had he been reading her mind? Sometimes, she thought, with a shiver of part fear, part excitement, that Eskoril could easily slip past cleverness into magic.

"Why? Well, because . . . because Roshan is awful. Everyone knows that. It is all heat and dirt and flies. Imagine having to live there – in a mud hut, I shouldn't wonder."

"How unlike my Princess to turn her back on an adventure because of a little discomfort."

Color flooded her cheeks. He had never spoken to her like this before. "It is *not* the discomfort. And I don't know why pigging it in a mud hut should be considered an adventure. It is more than that. Aunt Sankath wants to marry me off. And I won't."

He didn't seem surprised. "Do you disapprove of her choice, then?"

"I . . . I don't know who it is. It isn't that. I don't *want* to be married off. I want . . . I want to be free," she added lamely.

He didn't even *care* that she would have to leave Kamalant, that they might never see each other again, that she would have to marry . . . And she had thought . . . oh, how very stupid she was! She blinked back tears, her eyes on the white gravel at her feet.

"Princess, Princess," he chided and took her hands. "Come."

He led her to a carved stone bench under the shade of the

high wall at the farthest end of the garden. He sat so close to her that she could smell the *brakawood* perfume he always used and through it, faintly, the smell of horses. So he had had time enough to go riding in spite of "statecraft." Yet he had not invited her to go with him. Perhaps he had a new companion. The palace was full of beautiful women, older and more cunning, and Eskoril was without doubt the handsomest man at court. She pulled her hands away, suddenly furious.

"Antia, I need your help." His voice was gentle, almost pleading.

She looked up, startled. Eskoril was proud. He would never . . . "What can I do?" she asked, in spite of herself.

"Go to Roshan. For me."

Then that is it, she thought. He wants me out of the way. I *won't* let him see how I feel. "Why should I help you?" she asked coldly and stared past his shoulder at the pattern of leaves that shimmered against the wall.

"Princess, I thought we were friends."

She swallowed tears and hoped he had not seen the movement of her throat. "I thought so too, Eskoril. But friends are faithful, are they not? Friends do not play hot and cold."

"Ah."

His face was so hard to read. She sometimes felt that he only let people see what he wished them to see. Was that shame? Or sorrow?

"Princess, I have been your tutor since you came to the palace after the tragic death of your parents. Seven years. We have become close in those seven years." He took her hands again and held them firmly in his own. "My birth is not disgraceful by any means, Princess. But you are the heir to the throne of Kamalant and Komilant, and I am only your tutor. I am nobody."

"That's not imp . . . "

"Hush. It is a fact. And it is a fact that three ten-days ago we celebrated your sixteenth birthday. You are of marriageable age. And the Queen has the eyes of a hawk," he added softly. His thumb stroked the knuckles of her right hand. How large and strong his hands were. Hers were almost lost in their grasp.

She could feel happiness running through her body like a shower of gold, her face breaking out into a smile. "So that is why I have seen so little of you. I thought . . . "

"Did you not trust me, Princess?"

"Oh, Eskoril, I'm sorry. I've been sulking like a spoiled child. Of course I trust you. Truly."

"Then will you help me?"

"I'll do anything I can."

"Including going to Roshan?" The question was lightly put, almost in jest, but his pressure on her hands increased. Or had she imagined it?

Flies and dust and drought. She swallowed. "If . . . if it's really important, Eskoril."

The rare smile lit up his face. Her heart thumped against her ribs. "If your feelings for me are as mine are for you . . . " His voice was low. "But you must trust me completely."

"I do. Truly I do."

"Then go with the Lady Sofi. And write and tell me all that you see and hear while you are there."

"That is important? I don't understand."

"I said you would have to trust me. All I can tell you now is that I foresee a change in my fortunes. And when that has come about – when I am no longer a humble tutor – why then . . . " His eyes were dark and fathomless. "Why then, Princess . . . "

A strange prickling, like a sudden shiver, ran down her spine. She felt excited and scared at the possible future that suddenly seemed to open up in front of her. She had loved

14

Eskoril for as long as she could remember, but he had always been unattainable. She jumped to her feet to hide her confusion. "I will go to Aunt Sankath now and tell her that I have changed my mind, that I will go to Roshan."

His hand restrained her. "It would be wise if you seemed to be won over by her persuasion. If she were to suspect that you really *wish* to go then she might look further. She might seek out the person who had changed your mind."

"Oh, yes. And if she were to suspect it was you, and why . . . "

"She would have me executed for daring to approach the heir to the throne."

"Oh, Eskoril! I will be very careful. No one will even suspect, I promise you."

He kissed her fingertips lightly, then turned and snapped off a full-blown rose from a nearby bush. "Remember me in Roshan," he said softly. When she looked up from sniffing its fragrance he was gone.

He had not been there to see how cleverly she played her role at reluctantly accepting the Lady Sofi's invitation. He had not been at the palace during the turmoil of packing. He had not even been with the others at the harbor of Malan to see her leave.

He could at least have come to wave good-bye, Antia thought sadly. Then her hands gripped the railing. She would not feel sorry for herself. She had a job to do.

"Dry your eyes," she said briskly to the lamenting Nan. "Kamalant is quite out of sight and we'll see nothing more until landfall in Roshan."

"Nothing but sea serpents and monsters. You know what they say about the equator. On the other side everyone hangs upside down and the clocks move backward."

"Oh, Nan, what nonsense. The same sun and the same

15

stars shine upon Roshan that shine upon Kamalant."

"Bravo!" Lady Sofi's soft voice made Antia start. She had not heard her cross the deck. "It is up to us women to see that the friendship between Kamalant and Roshan is strengthened."

"Indeed, Lady Sofi," said Antia stiffly. She attempted a formal curtsey, but a sudden movement of the barque sent her staggering against the rail.

Lady Sofi laughed and steadied her with a firm hand. "Let us dispense with the formalities, certainly while we are at sea."

"Thank you, Lady Sofi." Antia looked guardedly at the woman by her side, the mother, doubtless, of the young man they wanted her to marry. What would she think if she knew that Antia had no intention of marrying her precious son, that the only reason she was going to Roshan was to help Eskoril?

Her thoughts made her uneasy – Lady Sofi was a very nice person – but she pushed her feelings aside. Eskoril loved her, that was the important thing. There wasn't any doubt, was there? Though he hadn't actually said . . . But she had given her word to help him and no feelings of loyalty to Lady Sofi or the Chief must get in the way of her skill at being his eyes and his ears. . . .

# 2

The royal barque crawled across the sea. There was not even the thrill of a storm or a meeting with a sea serpent to provide variety. Day after day Antia looked at the oil-smooth sea and the cloudless blue sky. Every night she lay in the small stuffy cabin beside the snoring Nan. The idea of helping Eskoril became less and less exciting, especially since she had no one with whom she could share this important secret. If she could have turned the sailing vessel around and headed back to Malan she would have done so joyfully.

But at last there came a morning when she was wakened from a restless sleep by a tapping at her cabin door. It was Lady Sofi, bright-eyed and lively, dressed in her spotless white robes.

"Huh?" Antia blinked awake.

"I know it's early," the other whispered, "but Roshan will be in sight at sunrise. It is something special I thought you might like to share."

So she splashed a little tepid water over her face, threw a shawl over her nightgown, and followed Lady Sofi up to the deck. In the bow it was almost cool. There was nothing to see but the dark blue of the sea reaching up to meet, at some indefinable place, the darker blue of the sky. The pale gleam of

17

phosphorescence curling back from the barque's prow was the only light.

"But. . . ?"

"Wait. Just wait."

Antia stared into the darkness. Then, quite suddenly, something seemed to leap up out of the sea ahead of them. A dark shape edged with gold like a heraldic symbol. Then from behind it the sun, like a huge red pomegranate, leaped up into the sky. The dark shape became a hump of land, breaking the line of the horizon, dark, featureless. Roshan!

"Breathe in deeply. Can you smell it? That is the scent of Roshan." Antia sniffed dutifully and got a whiff of aromatic spices overlaid with the smell of hot dust. She stared at Lady Sofi, whose eyes were suddenly filled with tears.

"You must think me very strange." Lady Sofi blinked and laughed unsteadily. "But Roshan is more than just my home. I know every rock and valley, every wadi and oasis, as I know the marks and wrinkles of my own body. Roshan's beauty is not obvious, but it stays with one forever. I hope you will learn to love it also." She put her arm lightly around Antia. In spite of herself Antia stiffened and pulled away. No, she was not going to be made to love this place nor its people. Never. Never!

"Run and get dressed, Antia," Lady Sofi said, as if she had not noticed her withdrawal. "I will meet you at breakfast."

All that day and the following night they approached the coast. Nan was not in the best of tempers, having to pack all their clothes in the heat of the tiny cabin. There had also been an argument with Lady Sofi.

"Let her wear something simple. We are a simple people, Nurse."

"I'm sorry, m'lady, but Her Majesty would have me whipped if I let the Princess go ashore looking less than her best." Nan's mouth folded so obstinately that Lady Sofi sighed and went away.

Very early next morning they docked at Lohat and after a last breakfast Antia followed the Lady Sofi on deck. She looked curiously at the stone quay, crowded with white-clad, brown-faced people, and up at the town, dumpy and mud-colored, its houses struggling up the hill. How . . . how provincial, she thought, and her lip curled.

The people below weren't waving or shouting or moving about, the way a crowd would in Kamalant. They stood quite still and each face was upturned toward the deck of the barque. The only things that moved were the green branches they carried.

Lady Sofi almost ran down the gangway, and as her foot touched the ground a single sigh went up, like a wind. Then the branches were waved overhead and dropped to the ground so that she stepped forward onto a carpet of greenery. She bowed to the people – bowed, thought Antia, unbelievingly – just as if she were their servant instead of it being the other way around. Everyone in the crowd bowed back, just bending their heads ever so slightly, not groveling on the ground or anything. Then they began to clap their hands softly, but there were so many of them that the sound was like the approach of a tropical rainstorm.

Antia felt unexpectedly shy in the face of this strangeness. She hung back, despite the grandeur of her best pink dress and the cap of gold embroidered all over with pink pearls. But Lady Sofi made it easy.

"And now friends, I bring you a guest: the Princess Antia of Kamalant." She stretched out her hands and Antia ran down the gangway and faced the crowd.

But I will not bow, she told herself. She smiled graciously and after a moment's silence there was a faint spatter of handclaps. She smiled again and waved her hand as Aunt Sankath had taught her.

Then they walked side by side across the green boughs that

19

covered the dusty ground to an open carriage at the end of the pier. It was drawn by a single lema, hardly different from the dusty, overworked beast she had seen pull the fruit cart down the road outside the palace in Malan.

I must ride in *this*? But Lady Sofi climbed up and she must follow her. The seats were dusty and she frowned. Her new pink gauze would be spoiled before she ever got to the palace. But it was necessary to sit and look pleasant as the poor lema dragged them up a steep cobbled street. Ahead a great wall of mud bricks was pierced by a wide arch.

"Is this the palace?"

"No, child." Lady Sofi laughed. "It is the entrance to the old city of Lohat. Our house – it is not really a palace at all – is at the top of the hill within the old city."

The carriage bumped and jolted up a steep winding road and at last stopped in front of a wall made of mud bricks set in a lacy design that left spaces between the bricks. Lady Sofi jumped down as a door in the wall creaked open.

There stood an old man, his face the same color as the brick, his skin as wrinkled as a dried nut. He smiled widely and she could see that he was completely toothless. Then he held out his arms and Lady Sofi ran into them.

Oh, no! Antia swallowed. Was this horrible old man Chief Hamrab? She got down carefully from the carriage, since it was obvious that the driver was going to make no move to help her, holding her dress so that it would not brush against the filthy wheel. Then she turned and curtsied stiffly to the old man, hoping that he would make no move to embrace *her*.

Then Lady Sofi was laughing and the old man too. "Antia, my dear, this is Thadron, who has known me all my life. He was the doorkeeper of my father's house and now he guards our home."

Antia felt her cheeks burning. How stupid! How could she have mistaken a doorman for the Chief? But why had Lady

20

Sofi not warned her? To cover her confusion she looked around disdainfully as Lady Sofi led the way through the arch. The courtyard was of beaten dirt, with no flowers or fountains. There was a covered well and beside it a trough where two women were washing clothes and shouting at each other in shrill, high voices.

"Come, Antia." Lady Sofi drew her out of the heat into a small dark hall, lit by a single smelly fish-oil lamp of brass that hung from the ceiling and by the light that filtered through the pierced brick of the walls. In the darkness at the back of the hall were five or six arched doorways, each covered with a bead curtain that swayed slightly in the small hot breeze that drifted through the sleepy house.

She jumped as a figure moved out of the shadows. Under the lamp stood an immensely tall man, lean, white robed, with a face hardened by sun and wind and deeply lined from the flared nostrils to the thin, stern mouth. Once she had seen him Antia knew, with no mistake this time, that this was the Chief of Roshan.

"Hamrab, I have brought Antia with me."

The hooded eyes lifted and she felt them pierce her. I would never dare keep any secrets from *this* man, she thought. Then she remembered her secret and Eskoril's and found herself blushing and unable to move, like a tongue-tied child instead of a princess.

The Chief crossed the hall and took her hands. His were calloused as if he were used to physical work. "You are welcome, Princess. My house is your house and my possessions yours."

She pulled herself together enough to curtsey and thank him in a voice that came out small and trembling. At that precise moment a young man burst through the curtains of one of the rooms, setting the beads jangling. He came to a stop when he saw her and grinned. He had a nice smile and his teeth were very white in a tanned face.

"Oh, so the dancing girls have arrived in Lohat already. How splendid! I wanted to arrange a ... "

"Jodril!" Lady Sofi's soft voice cut in sharply. "Come here and be introduced to our guest, the Princess Antia. My dear, this is my unruly son. Forgive his bad manners, bursting in on us like this."

Forgive? Never, never, thought Antia. To mistake *me* for a dancing girl. Her cheeks flamed. She allowed herself one more swift glance at the young man, whose hair, so blond as to be almost white, contrasted with cheeks that were even redder than hers. She nodded her head, gave the smallest possible curtsey, and turned away. "I am rather tired and hot, Lady Sofi."

"I will show you your room, my dear. This way." She lifted the bead curtain across one of the archways, and Antia walked into a room that was little more than a whitewashed cell. The side walls were of smoothed mud and the far wall, the outer wall of the house, was of the same patterned brickwork she had noticed earlier. Through it came light and air. There was no window. The furnishings consisted of two beds, two wooden chairs with seats and backs made of leather, and two chests, with a basin and ewer atop each. The walls were plain. There were no paintings, no silk hangings. Nothing but a shelf and half a ten of pegs to hang things on.

Antia bit her lip and anger burned inside her. Was this a deliberate insult to her, or worse still, to Kamalant? She wanted to stamp her feet and scream. She wanted to ... She took a deep breath. No, I am going to be very grown-up about this, she told herself. My visit is a matter of state.

"How pleasant." She forced a smile. How proud Eskoril would be of her acting. "So cool and ... and simple."

"Oh, I am glad you feel that way. I was afraid that ... but now I am even more sure that we have made the right choice. But enough of that for the moment." She sat on one of the beds and patted its edge, inviting Antia to join her. "I must confess to you that I missed our desert simplicity when I was away from Roshan. It is so good to be back."

Antia swallowed her anger. How casually this woman dismissed all the richness of Malan that had been offered to her during her stay at the palace. I will tell Eskoril, she thought. Perhaps it is important . . .

Where is he now? she wondered. Is he thinking of me and wondering how well I fare in this strange country? In her mind's eye she saw again his pale skin and dark compelling eyes. Even the memory of his limp made her heart beat faster.

Lady Sofi was staring at her, obviously waiting for a response. "I'm sorry. Forgive me. I didn't quite. . . ?"

"I was just asking you to try and forgive my son's manners and forget what he said. It was not deliberate rudeness, truly. Only a cultural misunderstanding."

"It is forgotten," Antia smiled. She burned inside. Dancing girls indeed! She would never forgive him, never.

"Good." Lady Sofi patted her hand and got to her feet. "I will leave you to rest. Your nurse should be here very shortly with your luggage. I am afraid you may find it a little difficult to store it all." She looked around the tiny room. "Might I suggest that you unpack only the most simple things. We live very humbly, by your standards. There is fresh water in the ewer if you would like a wash. Baths are more of a problem. Our fresh water supply depends on the rains and they have not been good for several years. But Jodril will take you swimming. You do swim? It is so pleasant to have the ocean almost at our door."

Alone, Antia wandered around the room, peering into the empty chests, bouncing on the bed, which was very hard, being but a wooden frame interlaced with strips of animal hide and overlaid with a thin mattress of wool. She tried to look between the bricks of the outer wall, but could see only sun and shadow. Just as well, or people might be able to see in. What a strange room it was, with no windows to see out of, a wall full of holes and a door that was not really a door.

Then Nan arrived, with four men sweating behind her with their boxes. She bossed them around, telling them where to place the luggage and then immediately changing her mind again. While she fussed, Antia stood as close to the pierced wall as she could, trying to catch the little breeze. Perspiration dripped down her spine and soaked the tight waistband of her pink gauze. It ran off her forehead into her eyes. I need a bath, with perfume and powder. I need servants with quiet voices and feet, not these hulking hod carriers!

At last they left, the beads jangling loudly, and Antia turned to vent her anger on Nan. But poor Nan had collapsed onto the nearest bed and was fanning herself desperately, her face crimson. Antia swallowed her anger. She stripped off her formal dress and tight slippers and kicked them into a corner of the room. Then, in her embroidered shift and under-drawers, she wrung out a towel in tepid water and patted Nan's face and forehead.

"Oh, thank you, dear pet. Oh, mercy, I shall never endure this heat. I shall die, I know I shall, and never see Kamalant again."

"You're too fat, Nan dear. Have you seen how thin the people here are? But don't worry. We'll stay no longer than we have to. Have courage."

"I don't know why you came in the first place, that I don't. I've never known you give way to your aunt like that before."

"Never mind that now. Just tell me in which box you packed my plain white muslin?"

"The one on the left. No, not that. The one next to it. But why in the world would you want it?"

"I shall wear it for dinner."

"Pet, the heat has addled your brains. That dress is for picnics, nothing more."

"It is what I intend to wear."

"Her Majesty would kill me."

"Luckily Her Majesty is not here. I only wish I had other dresses as simple. Well, you will have to wash and iron it each night, Nan, or find a girl you can trust to do it for you."

"Yes, Princess." Nan answered so meekly that Antia turned back to kiss the top of her head.

"It is not *you* I am angry with, dear Nan. Only . . ." But she couldn't even tell Nan that the young man they were scheming for her to marry had taken her for a dancing girl.

She went over to the box. At least the men had unstrapped it, but the heavy latches were a struggle. Within were layers of silver tissue paper, dresses carefully folded between each layer, the cap and matching slippers in embroidered bags among the folds. She dragged everything out until at the bottom – naturally it would be at the very bottom – she found the white muslin. She laid it on her bed and looked at it critically. It was so plain as to be laughable, hardly suitable for a palace servant. It would do. She poured a finger's depth of water into the basin and began to wash, scolding Nan as she did so.

"Get out of that dress and take off at least half of your petticoats, Nan. You'll be more comfortable after a wash too. And those shoes, no wonder you feel dreadful! Look how the heat has swollen your feet."

"I know the way a person of my class should dress, Highness," Nan answered huffily. "And I'll thank you to leave me to die in peace."

Antia laughed and dried herself on a small harsh towel. She slipped the muslin dress over her head, tied its sash, and sat down on her bed with the small carved writing desk in her lap. It had been her uncle's farewell gift. First she wrote a formal letter, addressed to their Supreme Majesties of Kamalant and Komilant.

*Dear Uncle and Aunt:*

*The voyage is safely over and we are at the home of Chief Hamrab and Lady Sofi.* She sucked the top of her pen and then dipped it into the inkwell. *It is extremely hot here and I do not have any correct clothes to wear.* She couldn't resist that snub to Aunt Sankath. *Lady Sofi sends you her greetings,* she guessed. *And I send you my dutiful love and fealty.*

*Your humble Antia*

There. That was done. She folded the letter and sealed it with wax from the little drawer in the desk and stamped the hot wax with her own signet ring.

She tossed the letter onto the bed and began to write to Eskoril. This was easy, just imagining that he was in the room with her and she telling him everything, as she had always done since he had first come to her as her tutor.

*. . . and I do not know if they really live in such poverty and meanness all the time, or if this is some kind of game – a way of testing me. But I intend to take whatever happens calmly and not seem to be surprised at anything they do.* She chewed the top of her pen again and went on. *I send this via the fast packet to Kamalant with my letter to my uncle and aunt. Is this how you wish me to continue our correspondence?*

*Your dear friend and pupil,*

*Antia*

She read it through, pleased with herself. She had left nothing out, nothing except that first meeting with Jodril. And after all his insulting words could hold no interest for Eskoril, could they? She folded the stiff sheets, sealed them, and clapped her hands for a servant. Nobody came. She went into the hall and called.

"Did you want something, my dear?" It was Lady Sofi.

"Oh! I just . . . I wanted to find a servant to take my letters down to the harbor. I noticed a steam packet there as we came ashore. If it hasn't left yet . . ."

"It will not have. How observant you are! Give me your letters and I will send a servant down to the harbor with them at once. I, too, have a letter of thanks to your royal aunt and uncle. They can go together."

There was nothing Antia could do but put her two letters into the outstretched hand. She bit her lip. Suppose Lady Sofi were to open the one to Eskoril? But why should she not write to her tutor if she chose? And the letter might not be flattering, but it did not reveal Eskoril's secret.

Lady Sofi was watching her with a most peculiar expression, almost as if she were laughing inside. "You are anxious to see the letters on their way, aren't you? Well, wait here for a second and I will fetch mine."

She vanished through one of the covered archways. The beads had not stopped swaying before she was back again, another letter in her hand. She could not possibly have had time to heat the seal, read the letter, and reseal it; not possibly.

"We will see if Negri is free to send the letters on their way." She called and a young boy appeared out of the shadows. "Take these to the harbor immediately, Negri, and give them to the Captain of the packet bound for Kamalant. Tell him to make sure that they are delivered to the palace at Malan as soon as they reach port. Matters of state."

Obviously impressed, the boy ran from the house. Lady Sofi's eyes twinkled as she turned back to Antia. "There, my

27

dear. I am sure that your special letter will arrive safely. Now, come and sit. What a charming dress. . . ."

For the first ten-days of her visit, Lady Sofi took Antia everywhere, to the smiths' market to watch them hammering the soft metal into bowls and flat plates, to the leatherworkers', where she saw leather stitched into bags and saddles as well as being made into furniture. In the rugmakers' quarters, men and women beat wet wool into flat sheets to become a heavy cloth used for both carpets and tent coverings.

"But I see no tents."

"Oh, they are used in the desert, in the heart of Roshan."

Something quivered inside Antia, a feeling that in that desert lay the secret of Roshan, the secret she was here to discover for Eskoril. She wasn't sure how she knew. Something in the tone of Lady Sofi's voice, or the look on her face, when she spoke of the "heart of Roshan." But she didn't know how to find out more, until one day luck took a hand. . . .

She and Lady Sofi were in the vegetable market early in the morning, before it got too hot, picking out dates and figs and pomegranates for lunch, when a sudden howling cry echoed through the narrow twisting streets. With extraordinary speed all the women pulled their playing children into the shadow of the doorways, the merchants swept their goods off the ground into sacks, rolled pots up in rugs, and pushed their tables back against the house walls.

Lady Sofi pulled Antia into the safety of an archway. "Stay well back," she warned her, as the howling cry came again, closer this time.

Antia tried to peer over her shoulder, but Lady Sofi blocked the view, almost as if she didn't want Antia to see what was happening. Quickly she ducked under the other woman's arm, ran forward, tripped, and fell into the street on her hands and knees.

From almost above her a warning shout rang out. She

looked up and screamed, her muscles suddenly turned to water. Great hairy legs ending in enormous padded feet strode toward her. As she shut her eyes, she was yanked back into the safety of the archway so violently that she thought her arm must be dislocated.

"Stupid child, how could you? You might have been killed." Lady Sofi's face was actually white with fright.

"My arm, oh, my arm." Antia hugged her shoulder.

"Did the *kroklyn* hit you? I thought I was in time."

"It was you. You did it. You need not have been so rough."

"There was every need. Look. And this time stay back."

A monstrous beast tore up the narrow street. Then another and another, crowding one behind the other, since the street was too narrow to allow more than one to pass at a time.

They were taller than the houses, these animals, with legs as long and sturdy as trees, with sinuous serpentine necks ending in small wedge-shaped heads. Their tongues lolled out over razor-sharp teeth and foam dripped from the corners of their mouths. The ground shook as they passed. The sky turned yellow with the dust in the air.

There were about twenty in all, each laden with panniers full of merchandise, each with a brown-robed figure balanced nonchalantly in the saddle. As soon as the last had passed, the street filled up again. The men pushed out their tables and unrolled their merchandise. The small brown children ran out to play their pebble games in the dust. The bargaining took up in midsentence just where it had left off.

White with fear and anger, Antia turned on Lady Sofi. "He should be whipped, that driver. I could have been killed. And they should not have been going that fast."

"Indeed you could have been killed. You must learn not to be so impetuous, Princess, when you do not understand. There was no time to explain. You should have trusted me."

"But I . . ."

29

"Once a desert-crossed kroklyn smells water no one can stop it. It is beyond control, like the *kamseen*, the great wind that tears across the desert, blowing where it will and stopping only when it chooses. You cannot stop it. You learn to bend to it. That is the whole secret of life in Roshan, my dear. The secret of being a desert people. To bend to the greater force — to bend but not to be broken."

Antia was in no mood to listen. Her knees still shook and she felt a little sick. "I want to go home. Right now!"

Back at the Chief's house she ran into her room where Nan sat fanning herself and gasping at the heat. "Nan, I was almost killed just now!"

"My pet! Oh, this terrible country! What happened?"

"It was a kroklyn. Have you ever heard of this beast before? It is the size of a house with legs like hairy trees. . . ."

"I told you the world would be different on this side of the equator, but you knew best. Now see. Nearly killed! Oh, pet, why don't you stay quietly in the shade as I do?"

"Because I would die of boredom."

"Then ride with young Jodril. Or go swimming. He's a lovely young man, my pet."

"How would *you* know?"

"Because he talks to me, that's why. He teases me too, but kindly. He said . . . " She spluttered with laughter and began to choke. "Oh, mercy me! He said he would teach me to swim. A lovely sight that would be, eh? Enough to bring the crowds out." She chuckled and wheezed. "But he's a lovely boy."

"I'd rather go shopping with Lady Sofi than go out with *him*." Antia's nose went up in the air. "He's so childish compared with . . . with people back in Kamalant."

Nan snorted. "Meaning that Eskoril, I'll be bound!"

Antia didn't hear. "Why, Nan, what's this?"

"What, my pet?"

"This letter. On my bed."

"Good gracious. How did it get there? I have been in here all morning."

"Sleeping, I'll be bound." Antia turned the letter over, examining the seal. It was not one she recognized. How could someone sneak in here and leave a letter, right under the nose of Nan, too? She shivered. This house gave her a creepy feeling. No locks on the doors – no *doors*, and what privacy was there in a bead curtain? The main gate was, of course, guarded by the ancient Thadron. But anyone with a mind to it could climb the wall and slip into the house and enter her room.

"Well, who is it from?" Nan asked eagerly. "A young man, I'll wager."

"Oh, Nan, what young men are there here?"

"There's Jodril."

"Him! Why would he write letters? He doesn't even talk to me when we sit next to each other at meals." She stood close to the wall of pierced brick where the light was better, broke the seal, and unfolded a single sheet of stiff paper. It was from Eskoril! She would know his writing anywhere. Her cheeks felt hot and she was thankful that her back was to Nan.

*Your description of life at the palace and in Lohat is complete. But what of the rest of Roshan?*

*In future you are to deliver your letters to me by leaving them in the care of the saddlemaker, Berron. You will find him at the last stall in the leather market. Be certain that no one sees you leave them.*

The letter was unsigned. There was no word of greeting nor suggestion that he might be missing her. Nothing. It was written as one might write to a servant. She crumpled the sheet in her fist, furious at the implied rebuke that she had not achieved much. Then she sighed. He was right to be disappointed in her. All this time she had been lazing about the markets with Lady Sofi, while outside the walls of Lohat a whole island continent waited to be discovered. . . .

She tore the letter into tiny pieces and poked them through the holes in the wall so that the breeze might take them. It would never do for Nan to see it. *And I won't let him down,* she vowed to herself. *I will find a way.*

At dinner that evening she set herself to be as charming as possible to Chief Hamrab. It was not easy. His bleak look, his powerful nose and piercing eyes, all seemed to strip the pretense from her. *If it were not for Eskoril I would never dare deceive him,* she thought.

"We saw a caravan today," she said, as casually as possible. "I wonder when it will go back to. . . ?"

"To Monar, I suppose. In a few days, I would expect."

"I would like to see more of Roshan than the city of Lohat. Though it has been most interesting," she added politely. "I'd like to accompany that caravan on its next journey to Monar."

"Oh, no," said Lady Sofi quickly.

"But . . . " said Jodril at the same time.

Antia's heart beat faster as she looked inquisitively from one to the other. *So there is something going on, something they do not want me to know. How clever of Eskoril.*

Chief Hamrab's eyelids lifted and he looked at her with a slight smile. "My dear, I do not believe that you could survive the rigors of a desert crossing. You are not Roshan-born."

His dark eyes actually seemed to laugh at her as they swept over her white and silver dress and her hair, curled and worn high, threaded with a silver ribbon. The white muslin had finally given out. *Oh, bother Aunt Sankath and her pretensions! He thinks I'm only a pampered child. I'll show him!*

Her chin went up and she stared at him boldly, though her hands, clasped in her lap, trembled. "I know my clothes are frivolous. My aunt chose them to impress rather than to be practical. But I'm sure Lady Sofi could find me something more suitable for a desert journey, could you not, Lady Sofi?"

"Well, I . . . "

"Quite impossible." The Chief shook his head.

Antia saw her advantage and laughed mockingly. "Oh, sir, do you really mean that Lady Sofi could spare me *nothing* to wear?"

"You are a minx, young lady!" Though his eyes twinkled, his face was serious. "I mean that such a journey would be too difficult for anyone not accustomed to it."

"Then I will become accustomed."

"You have led a sedentary life."

"Not always. I used to ride daily with my tutor and swim. Some years ago I took part in a scientific expedition into the great rain forest that divides Kamalant from Komilant. There were poisonous insects and snakes. We had to be covered from head to foot in spite of the heat to avoid the poisonous plants. And I was only twelve," she added triumphantly.

"Your aunt permitted you to go?" Lady Sofi gasped.

"She *encouraged* me. So you see . . ." She looked triumphantly from the Chief to his wife and intercepted a glance between them that puzzled her. A look of distress? It was obvious that they did not wish her to see more of Roshan than could be glimpsed from the high cliffs above the harbor. But there was more in that glance. Could it have been . . . pity? And why? Why should anyone pity *her*?

"My dear." The Chief suddenly spoke as adult to adult. "It might be politically unwise for you to go just now."

So. Antia traced the pattern on the tablecloth with one finger. "I must accept your judgment on that, Chief Hamrab," she answered formally. "But I would wish to return home on the next available ship."

"But why?"

"You have insulted me. Am I a friend or an enemy? It was

33

you who invited me to Roshan, not the other way around."
Her hand trembled and she tucked it back in her lap. In the icy
silence she could hear the low "pop-pop" of the fish-oil lamp.
An insect circled the lamp, around and around, until at last it
finally darted into the flame and fell to the floor with a tiny
rustle. The sweat trickled down her back and soaked the tight
waistband of her dress.

"Well, well." The Chief chuckled unexpectedly. "The little
kitten has claws after all."

She drew a shaky breath. Be careful, she told herself. Do not
relax. Then she found herself wishing she could play castles
with him. She felt sure that he would be better even than
Eskoril.

"Will you allow me to go, then?" she persisted.

"Not on this caravan. Perhaps on the next." As she relaxed
at his words and smiled, she felt a sudden easing of tension
somewhere else in the room. So who had been waiting for his
answer? Lady Sofi or Jodril?

"Thank you very much, Chief Hamrab."

He held up a warning hand. "*Only* if I can find you a suitable
guide and companion. That may still pose a problem. Obviously your nurse is completely unsuitable. What a pity that my
wife has affairs that must occupy her time for the next few
ten-days."

Lady Sofi blinked and then spoke quickly. "I *am* sorry, my
dear."

"Then who will it be? You must be able to think of someone
you can trust." It was maddening that the Chief should seem to
give way and then be "unable" to find anyone to go with her.
"Who?" she persisted.

There was a silence, and then, "What about Jodril here?"
The Chief smacked the flat of his hand on the table and beamed
at her.

Oh, no! Not him! Anyone in the world but him. Antia's

34

cheeks flamed. Then she saw, past the furious expression on Jodril's face, the fleeting smile pass between the Chief and Lady Sofi. So they were trying to trick her out of this trip.

She swallowed and managed to smile back. "Why, that would be wonderful. What an excellent choice. Thank you, Chief Hamrab. When may we start?"

# 3

The wind blew steadily out of the southwest, flattening her white robe against Antia's body. It whined ceaselessly against her ears and flapped and tugged at the scarf that swathed her head. The brown sand smoked around the sturdy legs of the kroklyns, at times reaching up to their knobby knees. They plodded onward in the half run, half shambling walk she had still not got used to.

The wind had begun to blow an hour after dawn, a dawn that had already seen them an hour's ride out of Lohat. It was getting on her nerves. She licked her lips. They were cracking already and, in spite of the cloth wrapped around her face, her teeth felt gritty. She shifted cautiously in the saddle and slid a hand between saddle and thigh. Ow, that hurt! How much longer would they ride today?

"Are you all right?" Jodril shouted above the wind. He was perched on the double saddle directly behind her. "We still have time to turn back. Only a half day's run to Lohat."

Antia's hands tightened on the saddle horn. "Of course I'm all right. What do you take me for? I've ridden for days across the savannas of Kamalant."

"A horse is not exactly the same as a kroklyn."

That it isn't, thought Antia, and tried to distract her mind

36

from the pain in her thighs and seat. She looked around, reminding herself yet again that they were south of the equator and that, though the sun was over their left shoulders, they were indeed traveling east. It would be hours before night fell. They had stopped only once, for a handful of dates and a swallow of tepid water. How much longer?

She looked across the interminable plain. Ahead plodded three kroklyns, each with a driver perched aloft and side panniers bulging. Behind followed two more. A small caravan, compared with the one she had seen in the market. She suspected that it might have been made up only to escort her to Monar and she wondered if the regular trade route lay on the way they would follow.

What was that? She blinked and saw a shimmer of water and a vertical shape in this flat land. Was it really . . . ? Yes, palm trees. "Oh, Jodril, look!"

"The oasis of Arrat."

"How far is it? I can't wait for a good wash."

He laughed. His irritating know-it-all laugh had been getting on her nerves ever since he was first ordered by his father to train her for this journey. "We'll be there tomorrow evening. And you'll get a bath if the kroklyns don't take all the water."

"Tomorrow *evening*? You're crazy! Why, it's right ahead, no more than . . . " She stopped. As their kroklyn crested a low ridge of hard-packed sand the image of trees and water shimmered and then broke up, like the reflection in a pool after you stir the water with your hand. Ahead lay nothing but an unforgiving stretch of hard claypan, broken into a million cracks and fissures by the cruel sun.

"Is all Roshan like this?" she wailed despairingly. "Nothing but dryness and illusions?"

"Oh, no. There are hills, and dunes that move like waves of sand across the land, and there are rocks and *handars* . . . "

37

"What are they?"

"Pillars of sandstone shaped by the wind into beautiful shapes, like sculptures. The desert people say that the wind gods carved them and that they are the entrances to their houses."

"But you don't believe that, do you?"

He laughed, embarrassed. "Oh, well, that is what is said. Then in the extreme east of Roshan there is a ridge of high mountains. Then there is the coast, as you have seen at Lohat. But of it all, this is what I love the most."

"This?"

"The space. The sky. Wait until you see it at night, a thousand million stars burning."

"The same stars that shine over Kamalant, I'm sure," she said dryly.

He shrugged. "You'll see."

The string of kroklyns shambled tirelessly on. There were no landmarks that Antia could see, but the drivers seemed confident of their direction. When they had been crossing sand she could at least look back at their trail and feel that they had accomplished something. Here on the hardpan the beasts' feet made no mark and she began to have the strange feeling that they were not in fact going anywhere at all. That they were on a treadmill. No matter how fast they went or for how long, nothing would ever change.

It was unbearably hot. She dozed. Her head fell forward and she woke with a jerk. It happened again. The third time she slumped over until her nose hit the high saddle horn. "Ow!"

"Are you all right, Princess?"

"Fine, thank you," she said with dignity, her hand nursing her nose. She bit her lip to keep awake.

At last their shadows began to run long in front of them and Jodril looked over his shoulder and then shook the reins. "Hold on."

"What's the matter?"

"We must be off this claypan before nightfall. It is a bad place."

As the kroklyn lengthened its stride Antia jolted in the saddle. She hung on grimly. I won't let him know how much I hurt, she told herself firmly. I *can* do it. I *can* make the crossing.

Ahead of them the other three kroklyns galloped and the two behind kept the same urgent stride. At length the claypan gave way to a scattering of rocks where they had to slow down. They scrambled up a low ridge. Beyond them stretched sand, rosy in the last rays of the sun.

"There. That is where we will sleep." Jodril pointed, and Antia looked around eagerly for an oasis or a wadi. But there was nothing but a great plug of red rock forcing its way up through the everlasting sand.

"Here?"

"Right here, close to the rock."

At Jodril's command their kroklyn stopped and lowered itself to its knees with a sudden forward and backward lurch. Antia forced her right leg over the hump of the saddle and slid stiffly to the ground. Her knees buckled and she grabbed hold of the kroklyn's coarse brown hair to steady herself. The beast grunted and the snakelike neck whipped around, greenish-gray teeth showing. Jodril smacked its neck and it turned away.

"Vicious beast. It should be muzzled."

"You'd snarl if someone tried to hang on *your* hair."

She was too tired to care that, once again, he had the last word. She slumped in the shade of the rock and leaned back. Jodril and the other five drivers filled pans of mush mixed with water and set them before the kneeling beasts. They slurped up the slurry quickly with soft tubular lips and when they were finished were given a pile of sweetcane to crunch.

Antia moistened her lips with a tongue that was almost as

dry. A ten-day ago she would have clapped her hands and demanded water, but she was learning. She might order it, but she would be ignored. The animals always came first. She sighed and shut her eyes. Her head throbbed.

"Water?"

She opened her eyes. A tin cup shimmered in front of her. She reached for it with trembling hands.

"Not all at once. Make it last. That's your ration for today."

She wet her lips and let the tepid water run around the inside of her mouth. She swallowed it drop by drop, with a sudden memory of the fountain in the courtyard of the palace in Malan. Water flowing on and on. Splashing onto the ground. Wasted. She could have cried.

She put the half-empty cup down carefully against the rock. Jodril came over with a tin plate. "Supper."

"This? Is this all?" A bunch of dates. A handful of ground-nuts. A cake of something unpleasantly gray. "What *is* it?"

"*Mishli*. It's very nourishing. We always travel with it. In fact its name means 'food for the journey.'"

"Yech! What's it made of?" She poked it.

"Eat it or leave it, Madam Princess. But you'll get nothing more."

She would have liked to throw the plate right into his stupid face and then walk away. But there was nowhere to walk to, and she was so very hungry.

She broke off a small piece of mishli and put it cautiously in her mouth. It was bland and sticky with a faintly sweet flavor. She managed to eat it all and then finished the dates and nuts. In very slow sips she drank the second half of her cupful of water. It wasn't really a meal. Perhaps Jodril was joking and soon there would be a plateful of *real* food. . . .

Jodril stretched and stowed away his plate and cup in one of the panniers. He threw her a blanket. "It'll be dark in a few minutes. Your bed, my lady."

40

She stared at him and then took the blanket, folded it in two and smoothed it out on the sand. She swallowed and blinked back tears. If she wasn't so tired and her head didn't ache, it wouldn't be so bad, but even on the expedition into the rain forest there had been servants along to pitch tents. There had been hot food and proper beds and . . .

She looked around in sudden despair. "Jodril, there is no bathroom."

He grinned. Oh, how he was loving this! "Around the far side of the rock, Princess. I will keep the men away until you return."

The sun set with dramatic suddenness in this wide un-lanterned desert world. She had to feel her way back around the rock to the place where she had spread her blanket. Jodril was already lying down, with the lumpy shape of the resting kroklyn close by. The beast smelled horribly.

"Can't you get it to move away?"

"We need it as close to us as possible."

"Why?"

"To protect us."

"From *what*?" Antia's voice went up. In the darkness Jodril chuckled. She bit her lip. He'd caught her out again.

"From the cold. What did you think? It'll be freezing just before dawn and kroklyns exude heat. If you wake up cold just snuggle up – to the kroklyn, I mean."

Antia snorted and climbed under her blanket. The sand was like a board against her hip and shoulders. After suffering for what seemed hours she sat up and painstakingly dug out hollows and piled the sand in a mound where her neck would be. She dusted off her hands, smoothed out her blanket, and lay down again.

That was a bit better. She rolled onto her back and looked up at the sky. It was thick with stars that blazed without a shimmer. A meteor flashed overhead and was gone. The stars seemed close enough to touch and yet at the same time to be infinitely far away. She felt as small as a single grain of sand on the rock that was Rokam. She could feel the curve of the planet beneath her, feel the wind of its turning against her face.

She wanted to shout for joy and to weep with loneliness, both at the same time, but the great silence prevented her. The silence was as large as the sky. It made her ears and her heart ache. She felt even smaller and more insignificant. Then, in another moment, it was as if she were in a great church whose wall was the red rock behind her and whose vaulted roof was the sky.

I don't belong here, I don't. She rolled onto her left side, curled up in a ball, one arm behind her head, the other wrapped around her knees. She shut her eyes tightly and willed away the vastness and the emptiness.

She woke up with the dawn sun flaming red in her eyes, while all around were the homely noises of yawning men and snorting kroklyns. The strange magic of the night might have been a dream. The reality was sordid and uncomfortable. She longed for a bath, for a toothbrush.

That day was almost a mirror of the previous one. Their caravan crossed an undulating plain of yellowish sand. By midafternoon the sand was studded with small thorny plants, each a man's stride or more from its neighbors. "See how cleverly they choose to live," Jodril pointed out. "Each one has enough and no more. They know that if they crowded they would all die."

"How *do* they survive?" Antia looked at the dry land.

"There is water underneath. It is not far to the oasis."

Antia strained her eyes, but when she first saw the palm trees in the distance she did not believe in them. Another mirage, she told herself. They won't trick me twice. But the kroklyn's stride lengthened. Its wedge-shaped head stretched out.

"It smells water. Hang on." Jodril's hard hands tightened on the reins. Antia clung to the saddle horn. Now the thornbushes were flying by. Beyond it Antia saw a saucer-shaped depression flooded with green, as if someone had carelessly spilled a pool of paint in the middle of the tan desert. There were zaramint bushes with their bright green berries. There were date palms, their tasseled tops stretching upward. And there was water! Not just one, but four stone-rimmed wells!

The kroklyn stopped so abruptly that Antia was almost pitched over its head. It flopped to its knees and its head snaked back over its shoulder, greenish teeth showing. It whinnied.

"Get down quickly. We must off-load so that they can go and drink their fill." Jodril flung himself to the ground and began to unstrap the panniers and saddle. Antia scrambled down just as the great beast struggled to its feet, shook itself, showering them with dust, and lumbered off to where a stone trough was being hastily filled by the other five drivers.

"If you're quick you can use the bathhouse before the men."

"But . . ." Antia looked helplessly around for her personal belongings among the bundles strewn everywhere. "A clean robe. My toilet things . . ."

"Off you go."

She ran toward the low stone building, her hot head jouncing at every step, feeling suddenly sick. But the bathhouse was dark and cool, smelling of dust and wet stone. As her eyes adjusted she saw the water-filled stone tank sunk in the floor. There seemed to be no taps, no drain. Dust scummed the surface. She looked back through the dark archway at the brilliant white outside, at the men struggling to control the fighting kroklyns around the water troughs. She hesitated. . . .

Then she flung off her clothes and plunged recklessly into the water. It was cold, wet, wonderful. She loosened her hair

43

and let it float out on the water. She ducked under and blew bubbles. If only she had soap and shampoo and sweet oil . . .

Don't be foolish, she scolded herself. Enjoy what you have. She lay back against the stone side with her eyes shut, simply soaking, until a warning shout from Jodril made her come to with a start and scramble out of the water. No towels. Nothing. Oh, well. She threw her loose robe over her wet body and tied the rope girdle about her waist. She leaned forward to squeeze the water from her long hair, and then walked reluctantly out into the white heat.

"Better?"

"Yes, thank you. It was marvelous. My headache's quite gone. But I wish I could find my toothbrush. I don't know which bundle it's in."

"You don't need a toothbrush." Jodril broke a twig from a zaramint bush and handed it to her with a flourish. She stared at it in bewilderment and he laughed, took another twig, stripped off the bark, chewed one end until it frayed to a brushlike tip, and then used it to scrub his teeth.

Honestly, thought Antia crossly. How primitive can you get! Any moment now one of these desert lemas will reinvent the wheel! But she had to admit that it worked very well and that the flavor of zaramint was fresh and clean in her mouth.

"You see?" Jodril looked unbearably smug. "Throw it away when you're through and next time pick a fresh twig. Much nicer than putting a brush in your mouth time after time. Ugh!"

Antia flushed and turned her back. It was infuriating of Jodril to be right so often. She found a shady place beneath a group of palms and dozed until she was wakened by the delicious smell of cooking. I don't think I've ever been as hungry in my whole life, she thought, and waited impatiently until at last Jodril came over to her with a mug of hot vegetable soup and a plateful of small cubes of savory meat that had

44

been roasted over the fire on sticks. The meat was sweet and tender, tangy with woodsmoke.

"It's marvelous. What is it?"

"Don't ask. Just enjoy it."

"Oh, for goodness' sake stop teasing me, Jodril. It's becoming very annoying."

"Well, then, if you must know, the meat is a mixture of *slimas* and *karlas*, chopped into pieces and grilled. Real desert fare."

Antia felt the blood drain out of her face. Her stomach heaved. Slimas! They were the small desert snakes that flourished everywhere in wadis and oases. Quite harmless, she had been told. As for karlas, they were pretty little tree lizards with red lozenge shapes on their sand-colored skin, that lived on dates.

No wonder the meat was sweet. She swallowed desperately and managed to hold back a shudder. She went on eating, aware that Jodril was watching her. She forced herself to clear her plate.

"Let me get you more," he said solicitously.

"I couldn't manage another piece. Thank you. It was delicious." She handed him her plate and then bolted for the bushes, sweat breaking out on her face. When she got back, he was grinning from ear to ear, though he said nothing, just handed her a cup of water.

"I think I'll sleep," she said. Anything to get him out of the way.

"It's early yet. There will be tales and songs around the fire. Wouldn't you like to. . . ?"

"I'd sooner sleep."

"As you wish." He shrugged and walked away to join the drivers. She could hear their voices going on for hours, laughter and the rattle of bone dice. Their fires glowed and crackled cheerfully and Antia felt horribly alone. But I won't be friends, she told herself firmly. Not with *him*. Not ever.

The third day passed at last and the fourth. It was on the afternoon of the fourth day, as they crossed a plain broken by wind-carved dunes, that the sky darkened as if a bank of clouds had suddenly covered the sun.

They looked behind them. The sky was a dirty brown and the sun glowed dully.

"Is it going to rain?"

"Would that it were. No, it's a dust storm, a bad one by the look of it, to come up so quickly. We'll have to stop and take shelter."

"Shelter? Where?" Antia looked around at the undulating curve of bare dune. There was not even a thornbush in sight.

"Hang on." Jodril kicked and turned the kroklyn and maneuvered it into a circle, nose to tail with the others.

"Slide down on the inside," he ordered Antia, as soon as all six beasts had knelt.

She crouched out of the way as the drivers rapidly tied lengths of cloth from saddle to saddle across the circle of kroklyns until they had made a rough roof. It was like being in a warm furry cave, the walls of which were the shaggy sides of the animals. Each beast had tucked its head into the circle against its flank, so that in the semidark she could see twelve eyes glaring balefully. It gave her the shivers, though the men squatted comfortably on their haunches, joking to each other in a dialect so thick that she could hardly make out a word.

Above them the cloth suddenly shivered. Within the "cave" it was hot and very smelly. "How long will we have to stay here?" she asked Jodril.

He shrugged. "The wind is the master and we are its servants. It may be only a few hours. Perhaps days."

"Days! Wouldn't it have been better to have outrun the storm?"

"Outrun? Closer to Monar I can show you the bones of strangers who thought they could outrun the wind."

The wind's voice shrilled to a scream. It went on and on, driving into her head. Sand spattered over their heads with sudden viciousness. It was terrifying. She covered her ears and crouched against the warm flank of the kroklyn. Oh, Eskoril, why did you persuade me to come here? What am I doing? I'm going to die in the midst of this terrible sand and I won't have done one single useful thing.

The drivers seemed to be arguing with one another, their voices raised against the wind. Now and then she caught them looking at her, and their faces were not friendly.

"What are they saying?" She pulled Jodril's arm.

"Nothing special." But he looked uncomfortable.

"They are so. It's about me, isn't it?"

"Just driver talk. Nothing more."

She listened to the dialect and caught the odd phrase. "The Great Dune is angry . . . " "As long as *she* is here . . . "

The Great Dune? Jodril had not spoken of such a place in his lessons about their trip. Perhaps she had misunderstood. Then she noticed that Jodril had loosened the ornamental dagger that he wore in the binding of his robe. He now sat with his right hand resting casually upon its hilt.

Oh, Eskoril, I wish you were here to help me. What use is this *boy*? She made herself as small as she could against the kroklyn's side and did not move or talk anymore. If only I were back at home, she thought. If only . . .

At last the wind dropped to a low whine. She felt that they had been there for hours and she was surprised to see daylight when the men loosened the cloths above them. The kroklyns raised their heads and sneezed sand from their nostrils.

"Is it over at last?" Antia dared to whisper.

"Perhaps. We cannot be sure. Often the wind comes back again from another quarter. We won't travel any farther today anyway. See, the kroklyns know. They're not getting up."

"Perhaps they're just lazy. Look, there's blue sky over

47

there." Antia scrambled onto the back of their beast and from the vantage point of the saddle looked around.

It was a strange sight. On the windward side the sand had been blown up over the panniers almost level with the backs of the kroklyns. The way they had come was smooth as if the world was new made, blasted clean of every sign of human passage.

Well, at least I have survived a sandstorm and that is something! In spite of eyes that stung with sand and wind, in spite of the sand gritting between her teeth and itching in her nostrils and ears, Antia felt excited. She slid down the kroklyn's far side. Luckily their beast had been on the leeward of the storm, but even so she sank almost up to her knees in loose sand.

"Stay close by," Jodril warned. "Remember, after the blow comes the second blow."

"Yes, yes." But she wasn't really listening. Oh, how good it was to stretch and to be free of the smell of kroklyns and the fierce glances of the drivers. She walked downwind to where a ridge of hard-packed sand rose ahead of her. From its crest she would have a great view of the half-buried caravan and of the waves of dune after dune, like a frozen ocean.

As she reached the top her robe suddenly fluttered, like a sail catching the wind. She turned. The wind was blowing again from a different quarter, ahead and a little to the right. The sky was darker again and the sand was a strange reddish color. She looked west. The sun was low in the sky, huge and as red as a pomegranate.

Jodril was calling and waving. She was just about to return when a movement caught the corner of her eye. What was it? She stared across the sea of dunes. There was a ridge, rising high above the others, and atop it a huge shadow loomed. It was an enormous shape, but human. If it straightened, she found herself thinking in fear, it would touch the sky.

48

What was it? Jodril's tales came back to her. The god of the wind ... of the desert. Antia's dry lips parted and she screamed. The noise she made shocked her back to reality. It's nonsense. I don't believe all that Roshan superstitition, she told herself.

Then the figure did straighten up and became the size and shape of an ordinary human being. One hand was raised as if it were beckoning. Behind Antia, Jodril called again. His voice was torn to rags by the rising wind. She should go back. But who was this person? Perhaps the person was lost, or needed help. Or perhaps – a small voice spoke inside her – perhaps it had something to do with the secret of Roshan.

It's only the next dune, she told herself as she began to scramble down. I can't possibly lose myself. New sand rose under her slipping sandals. From the valley floor the next dune reared up, long and high. She began to scramble up it. Over her shoulder the sun set in a bloody welter. The landscape took on a nightmare appearance.

She clawed and scrambled her way to the top of the dune where she thought she had seen the figure. It was deserted. The ridge stretched in a sharp curved line to right and left. She was completely alone. But someone had been there. She had seen someone. There would be footprints. She bent to look. There was nothing, nothing but her own. As she stared at them the wind casually rubbed them out.

Fear thumping in her chest she began to run down the side of the dune. She slipped and rolled down to the valley. She picked herself up and scrambled up the side of the next dune. From the top she would be able to see the circle of kroklyns. She would be all right then. From the top of the next dune she stared. There was nothing but sand and more sand, undulating in every direction.

She tried another dune, a little to the right. And then another. At last the wind drove her back into the valley. Dust

49

blinded her and sand peppered her hands and feet like shot. She tripped and fell again, struggled to her knees and looked around. Ahead of her was a faint, ghostly shape. She crawled toward it.

What was it? She stretched out a hand and felt a stab. A snake? She didn't know that she could be more afraid, but now she was. She stared at the small drop of blood on her palm and then forced herself to move forward again. It was a bush, that was all, low, thin-leaved with long silvery thorns. She crouched in its lee, though it gave little enough protection, and she pulled her headcovering right over her face, leaving just the smallest space through which she might breathe.

The wind thrummed in her ears and battered at her crouched body. Outside the small tent of her robe it grew dark. At length something strange began to happen. Though the wind blew on she no longer heard its voice. She no longer felt the sand beating at her body, nor the hard ground under her knees. The storm emptied her mind and blew it away. It was as if Antia, Princess of Kamalant, heir to the throne of the twin continents, had ceased to be.

# 4

Instead of the burning heat she became slowly aware that she was very cold. Her eyes opened reluctantly to a profound darkness. Was she blind? Had the storm done that? Her invisible hands brushed her face, her eyes . . . she could not tell. A spasm of fear shook her. Perhaps this was death. She shut her eyes tightly against the dark and the aloneness.

Later she opened them again and saw a flicker of light. It was not blindness! She turned joyfully toward the source. Then fear again tightened her chest so that she could hardly breathe. The light was coming from a small dark lake, a lake so dark that its substance seemed like the darkness that surrounded her. Flames danced like ghosts across the surface. She struggled and tried to scream and someone held her tightly.

Her next experience seemed to come later, as if she had been sleeping or unconscious. Strong hands held her, cradled her in cool water. She was weightless and there was no more pain. Water trickled down her parched throat, was sponged over her dry lips. She tried to speak, but could form no words. Only an ugly sound like the croaking of a swamp frog broke the silence.

Silence. She slept again and awoke to silence. She had thought she had gone blind. Now she wondered if she were deaf. She strained her ears and heard a single musical note. Another and another. Faint and regular. After a long time she worked out what it must be. The sound of water dripping from a height.

Wonderingly she opened her eyes. Light danced everywhere. It was reflected off a vaulted roof of rock, off wet pillars of rock. Off the walls, where it seemed that water had flowed and hardened into a pattern of rippling draperies. Wherever she looked the light flashed back in unexpected jewel bursts of white and gold and red.

She lifted her head and saw that the light originated from three torches of wood held upright in iron sconces fastened to the walls. Their flames rose and fell on hidden gusts of air, and they burned on and on, never dimming or being burned away. She felt as if she were lying in the heart of a hollow crystal made entirely out of light except for the darkness that lay at the very center.

What was the darkness? It drew her eyes insistently. She struggled up onto one elbow and saw a small lake, as deep and as dark as night. It was still, as if it had lain there untouched since the beginning of time. Still . . . except that after she had watched it for a long time she became aware that near its dark and secret heart a faint tremor shook its surface. The pool was of living water.

The stillness spread a peace right through to the center of her being. Her eyes closed. Just before she drifted into sleep she thought: If I *am* dead, it is really very nice.

Fingers dug into her shoulder, hurting. Hands shook her. She heard the same words repeated over and over again. At last they made sense. "Antia, please wake up. Please, please wake up."

She obligingly opened her eyes. Jodril's face was just above hers. It was drawn and he looked unexpectedly older, a man rather than a youth.

"You are alive! Shudi said . . . but you looked so . . . I wasn't
sure."

"What . . . ?" Her voice was a croak, as if she hadn't used it
for a long time. He held her up and gave her a drink of water,
cold and sweet. It stirred a dream memory. "Where am I?"

She looked around at a room carved out of golden sandstone. The bed on which she lay was carved out of the wall.
There was no window. What light there was filtered through a
doorway, whose round arch was reinforced with bricks. The
floor too was of brick. Half house, half cave. Memory stirred
again. Or perhaps it had been a dream.

"I'm alive! I really am." She swung her feet off the bed shelf
and then stood up carefully. "Why, I feel great!"

Jodril jumped to his feet and grabbed her shoulders. His face
suddenly flushed. "You stupid little lema." He shook her.
"What do you mean by running off like that? I *told* you the
wind would be back. I warned you. I called." He shook her
again until her teeth rattled. Then his hands dropped to his
sides and he stared at her, the color fading from his cheeks.
"How did you live? I don't understand. In that storm . . . you
should be dead. And how did you get *here*? All the way from
the northern dunes to Ahman . . . even without the storm you
could *never* have found your way."

She ignored his questions. "Don't you *ever* do that to me
again, Jodril." She blinked back tears of rage and pain. Her
chin went up. "You forget who I am."

"Much chance I have of forgetting that, your Imperial
Highness! With your stupid clothes and your queenly
manners, always turning up your nose at the food or the water
or . . ."

"You're a fine one to criticize. You may be the son of a chief,
but you act like a kroklyn driver. You've never once tried to be
friends, ever since I got here. It's not much fun being stuck in a
strange country with no one I can really talk to but Nan."

53

"Oh, yes. And what if I had acted friendly? You'd have thought I was as anxious to marry you as your uncle and aunt."

"Marry? Why, I'd sooner marry a kroklyn driver than you."

"And I'd sooner marry a fisherman's daughter and live on a leaky boat for the rest of my life."

"You are the most insulting person I have ever . . . "

"So now you're pretending you don't want to marry me. Lying again. You're always lying!"

"I am not."

"All those stories about your fancy palace and your garden and your baths and . . . "

"But it's the truth. Kamalant *is* the most beautiful country in the world and that's the truth. And I am *not* going to marry you, and that's the truth too."

"You're not lying?"

"I AM NOT LYING!" Antia shouted at the top of her voice. "I only came to Roshan because my aunt made me." She hooked her thumbs behind her back. After all, it was almost the truth, and she certainly couldn't tell Jodril, of all people, why she had really come to Roshan. "But even though she made me come, she can't make me marry you, and I wouldn't, not if you were the last man in Roshan, so there!"

A sudden peal of laughter made them both jump and turn. A tall, thin woman, dark-skinned and with the blue eyes of most Roshanites, stood in the archway, her hands on her hips.

"I can tell that you are much better, little one. I could hear your voice right across the courtyard. As for you . . . " She turned to Jodril and the corners of her eyes wrinkled with amusement. "Is this the lad who came in here wringing his hands and weeping because he had lost his little friend?"

Jodril's face flushed. "You don't understand," he spluttered. "If anything had happened . . . well, my father would have killed me. After all, she was in my charge."

"I see." The woman's blue eyes twinkled infuriatingly. "Do

54

you have any more quarreling to do? Or do you wish to become friends and break bread at our table?"

"Oh, I am *starving*." Antia moved toward the doorway. The woman's arm barred the opening. "You may not share food while a quarrel hangs between you. That is the desert way."

"Oh." Antia's stomach rumbled. She swallowed. "Well . . . look, Jodril, if you'll apologize for shaking me like that and saying all those rude things, then . . . "

"And how about you apologizing to me for being so stupid and disobedient, running away into the storm like that?"

"I didn't know what was going to happen, did I?"

"I told you . . . "

"I didn't hear . . . well, actually I did hear but I thought you were playing the little chieftain again. And I really was afraid of the drivers."

"They were just sand-happy. It'd have come to nothing."

"Then why did you draw your dagger. I *saw* you, Jodril."

"Well . . . " Jodril drew his breath and let it out again. "Look, if you really don't want to marry me, and if you can believe I don't want to marry you either, then why don't we forget about the past, right up to this minute. Let's start all over again and be friends."

Antia hesitated. She *needed* that apology.

"Well?" asked the strange woman, her hand still on the door arch.

I'll never get a meal if I don't make up, and I'm starving, she thought. "Oh, very well. We'll start over again."

"Shake hands on it, then." Jodril held out his hand and she took it reluctantly.

"Come." The woman led them into the front room of the cave. This was furnished with two sitting shelves piled with rugs. There was a low table made of thornwood and leather, and fat leather cushions were scattered on the brick floor.

Light lay in a dappled pattern across the bricks and blazed white beyond another archway, whose wooden door stood open.

Antia stepped through into the open air beyond and cried out in surprise. Instead of the simple courtyard, surrounded by a wall of burned brick, such as was commonplace in Lohat, this house opened onto a courtyard sunk ten metres or so beneath the ground. The whole house was underground. She looked up past walls of sandstone smoothed and shaped about the entrance through which she had come, more roughly hewn higher up, to a blue sky far above. On two of the other walls surrounding the courtyard were entrances similar to the one through which they had come. In the fourth wall was a wide, high arch, with a wooden door swung open in two halves. Beyond it she caught a glimpse of a flight of wide and shallow steps carved out of the rock.

"Sit, sit." The woman indicated chairs, woven of hide on frames of thornwood, grouped about a stone slab table supported on boulders. She bustled away, leaving them standing awkwardly, not looking at each other.

"Well, we may as well do as she says," Jodril indicated a chair in the shade of one of the two massive trees that grew in the courtyard and rose to the level of the ground far above.

"What did you say this place was called?" Antia asked as she sat down.

"Ahman. The oasis of Ahman lies about a thousand paces to the south. That was where we were bound for before the storm struck."

"Where are the drivers and the kroklyns?"

"At the oasis. We went directly there once the storm was over. Then I came here to ask for the help of the villagers. To ask them to help me find your . . . your body."

"But I was already here, alive and well?"

"Yes."

56

"Jodril, how did I get here? How far would it be?"

"An hour's walk or more, for someone who knew where they were going."

"So the people here brought me in?"

Jodril shook his head. "Shudi said that her husband, Atmon, found you slumped against the door as soon as they opened it."

"And that's all?"

"Don't *you* know what happened?"

"I don't think so. I remember losing my direction and running . . . "

"But why, Antia? Oh, don't bristle up like that. I'm not trying to start another fight. But why did you go off in the other direction after I called you?"

"Let me think. I don't . . . yes, I remember now. It was the strangest thing, Jodril. I was coming back, honestly I was. Then I saw this huge shape with its arms lifted up. Then it turned and I swear I saw it beckon to me. So I followed. *Then* I got lost."

"It must have been a *wrytha*." Jodril's face paled.

"What's that?"

"Like a ghost, there and not there."

Antia tried to laugh. "I thought that was a mirage."

Jodril didn't smile. "The mirage of a giant figure beckoning. If you follow you will die. There is a saying in Roshan: The wise man shuts his eyes to the wrytha. Meaning that it's stupid to go looking for trouble."

Antia laughed uneasily. "I don't believe in ghosts leading you to your death. It's not scientific."

Jodril shrugged. "Then what was it?"

"I don't know. But I . . . I don't want to believe in wrythas."

"I don't like the idea of them too much myself. Anyway, what happened next?"

"I began to run after the figure. I think . . . yes, I remember I

57

had the idea that whoever it was might be in trouble. I thought maybe I could lead him back to the kroklyns before the storm struck again. But I fell and lost my direction. All the dunes looked alike. Then I fell over a thornbush and pricked myself. I remember the blood. I was scared it was a snake."

Jodril caught her hand and turned it palm up. "There's nothing there."

She pulled her hand away. "It was just a prick. But it bled. I remember spots of blood falling on the sand. And blood on my robe."

"You were dreaming. There's no blood."

"But I remember perfectly. Later I think I dreamed, but not then. The pain shocked me and made me think. I stopped running and crouched down by the bush and covered my head. It was unbearably hot and dry. Every breath choked me. I remember *that*."

"But not how you got to the village?"

"No."

"It makes no sense. I wonder if Shudi is hiding something."

"Does it matter?" The heat was making Antia sleepy.

"It's a mystery and mysteries are always important, don't you think? Why, what did I say?"

"Nothing." Antia had sat bolt upright and was staring at him. A mystery! "Nothing at all. Go on."

"Well, the point is that no one outside the village could have found you and brought you here, and yet . . . " He stopped in midsentence, his mouth open.

"Whatever is it? You look quite sunstruck."

"Nothing. I mean, that's the mystery, isn't it? Nobody from the village brought you. You must have come alone."

And that "no one" took me into the dark and washed me and healed me and brought me here, thought Antia. Yes, it is a mystery. . . .

Then Shudi bustled out of the cave house with flat cakes, hot and crisp, a dish of mashed beans and a bowl piled high with dates. They fell on the food and talked no more until the plates were empty.

"Oh, that was good." Antia sat back with a contented sigh. "And the best is the water. It tastes so good. It reminds me . . . "

A sudden babble interrupted her as a horde of children, accompanied by ten or so older people, poured down the stairs and into the courtyard. They were all talking at once.

"What is it? What's happened?"

Jodril looked vexed. "They've been over to the oasis to pick up news. They say that the drivers have gone on to Monar without us."

"What!" Antia jumped up. The children, who had come close to see the strange girl, tumbled over each other to get out of her way.

"Don't worry. They'll be back in six or seven days."

"But that's no good. I didn't come to Roshan to sit in a hole in the ground for seven days. You're the son of the Chief. Can't you do something? Why did they leave anyway?"

"They thought you were bad luck." Jodril's voice was serious, but the muscle at the corner of his mouth twitched.

She stamped her foot. "It's not funny!"

"They're only ignorant Roshanites, Your Highness."

"Don't start that again. I thought we were going to be friends."

"It was you stamping your imperious foot that set me off. Sorry. Antia, we'll have to make the best of it, that's all. I dare say that time will pass quickly. And at least the drivers left our bundles. Here is yours."

"Well, thank goodness for a change of clothes. Will Shudi do my washing if I offer to pay her?"

"She'd be insulted if you offered her money. And she's

59

very busy with her children and the old people. Couldn't you do it yourself?"

"Don't be silly. I don't know how to wash clothes."

"It'd pass the time," he said odiously and vanished with his bundle into the darkness of one of the other houses.

If I weren't a princess, thought Antia savagely, I'd . . . I'd hit him!

But later, when Antia saw Shudi smacking the family wash against a flat stone and scrubbing the dirtier bits with another stone, she decided to wash her own after all. There was no soap, but she rinsed everything in a small pail of precious water, which then watered the tree, and hung them to bleach and dry in the sun.

After Jodril left, Antia took her own bundle into the house and unpacked her box of creams and face paint. With her jewel box and her traveling writing desk on the shelf above her head, she felt more at home.

"Antia!" Jodril's voice called from outside.

"What is it?" Was he still playing games with her?

"Are you tired, or would you like to go up to see the sunset?"

"Oh. Oh, yes, thank you." She followed him eagerly up the staircase that led, in two flights, from the level of the house up to the ground. The upper walls, she noticed, were encased in brick to hold back the looser sand that must lie above the rock, and she wondered who had carved the caves and laid the brick. She asked Jodril, but all he could tell her was that they were very old.

The top of the stairs faced west and her first sight was of a blood red sun close to the horizon and a sky flushed a warm rose. "It's beautiful."

"It's always so after a bad dust storm. Roshan takes, but she always gives in return."

"You talk as if Roshan were a person, not just a piece of ground to be used and lived on."

60

"That is how we think of her."

To the west the dunes rolled like a sea under a low swell. To the south the desert stretched flat. You would never guess that a house lay under the ground. Only the telltale shadows made by the sinking sun showed the walls around the hidden courtyard. She leaned over. From up here she could almost touch the topmost leaves of the trees. She could hear faintly the laughter of the children. Then she looked south again, and saw other walls, squared about other courtyards. "Why, it's a whole village underground!"

"A very small village. Ten families. That is all that there is water enough for. Though there is more in the oasis." He pointed south.

"Let's go and see it."

"It's a twenty-minute walk. The desert light makes everything seem closer than it is."

"I'd like to go anyway."

"It's no different from the oasis of Arrat. But if you want . . . "

He was right. There was a grove of date palms, with scrubby undergrowth and a few tough grasses. There were two covered wells and a brick bathhouse. The acrid smell of kroklyns still lingered on the air. After a few minutes they turned to walk back.

The sun was just setting and its last rays threw into strong relief the sculpting of the dunes that lay to the north of the village. One dune, directly beyond the village, was the largest Antia had yet seen. It lay, like a beached sea monster, its tail merging with the flatter desert floor, its great shoulder heaved up against the sky over to the northwest.

"How wonderful. What a view we could get from the top." She quickened her pace, but Jodril held her back. "It'll be dark long before we get there and there'll be nothing to see."

"Tomorrow, then," she agreed amicably, though she had a feeling that his real reason for holding her back was something else.

The next day, Jodril said it was too hot for climbing during the day. "All right. This evening," Antia said as patiently as she could.

But when evening came the meal turned into a storytelling session that went on and on until long after sunset. It would have been interesting if she had been able to follow the stories, but the villagers spoke a dialect so broad that Antia could understand only a few words. It was maddening to listen to the laughter and not to have understood the point of the story. The music which followed was not much better, a droning on two gourd pipes that went on and on with very little tune that she could detect.

Tomorrow, she vowed, as she tried to sleep on the hard stone slab, with only a single fur between her and the stone, tomorrow I will climb that dune and find out what secret lies beyond it.

She waited and watched. In the late afternoon Jodril went indoors with one of the children. At once she slipped quietly out of the courtyard and ran up the long flight of stairs that led to the desert. The sun was still hot enough to slow her down to a walk. Her shadow fell long to her right as she trudged over sand that was as hard as iron. The Great Dune was farther away than she had expected and she was hot and out of breath by the time she reached its base.

It was not one of the drifting dunes that marched across the desert ahead of the prevailing westerlies, she realized. It must have been stable for a very long time to have grown to its present size. The sand was firm on the lower slopes and walking was not difficult, but the gradient was steep and she had to stop every few minutes to catch her breath.

"Antia, wait! Antia, come back! You mustn't . . . "

There was a sound of panic in Jodril's voice that made her stop and turn instead of ignoring him.

"You mustn't climb the Great Dune," he gasped as he caught up with her. He must have run the whole way. "It's sacred to the desert people."

"You could have told me honestly instead of making excuses."

"It's a . . . secret. We know of it but we don't talk about it. That's all."

"Well, I still think you could have said something. Now I'm horribly hot and covered with sand for nothing. You're hopeless, Jodril."

She stalked back to the village ahead of him and sulked for the rest of the day.

*. . . and I'm not sure I believe him,* she wrote in her diary the next morning. *Though it's perfectly true that one of the drivers said something about the Great Dune just before the second storm. But Jodril wasn't telling the truth. People do go up there. I saw a footprint on the ridge just above me.*

She turned over the page and sucked her pen thoughtfully.

*I know there is something that Jodril is trying to hide from me. I'm not sure about the others. Except for Shudi they are so hard to understand, and sometimes she doesn't answer when I ask her things. I don't know what Eskoril wants, but there is something strange going on. What have I found out so far?*
*1. The Chief and Lady Sofi didn't want me to go to Monar. They only changed their minds when I threatened to go home.*
*2. Jodril was upset inside about the drivers leaving us here, though he made light of it at once. Why?*
*3. Maybe he didn't want me to stay at Ahman for a ten-day. Maybe the secret of Roshan, whatever it is, has something to do with this place.*

63

*4. The Great Dune is definitely part of it. But what?*
*5. Whatever happened to me in the storm is part of the secret,*
*too. Jodril asked me so many questions. Then he got an idea and*
*he wasn't curious anymore and didn't want me to be either.*

She stopped writing and chewed her pen again. Eskoril
would be proud of me, she thought. But I wish I could
remember exactly what happened to me after the storm.
Perhaps if I wrote it all down it would be clearer in my mind.
She began to scribble again.

*I do remember being carried into a place that was cold and very*
*dark, not a house, but a cave. But not like the house-caves of*
*Ahman. There were stalactites and stalagmites and water*
*dripping softly into a pool. Cool sweet water. Someone bathed*
*me in it. . . .*

And *that* is why there was no blood on my robe, she thought
triumphantly. I wasn't dreaming! It was washed off in the
pool.
There was something else, something scary, that she didn't
want to remember. Could it really have happened? It was
more like a nightmare. She bit her lip and then began to write
again.

*It was just after I woke up in the dark. There was a pool. I*
*don't think it had anything to do with the other one. It was in a*
*much smaller cave. But the water was on fire.*

There. Eskoril would probably laugh at her, but she had
honestly written everything she could remember. Once she
got back to Lohat she would write a long letter to him, telling
him everything she had put in her diary.
Just then Shudi called her to lunch, and she left her writing

desk and diary on the chair beneath the tree. Lunch as usual was dates and fried flat cakes. She sighed. How pleasant it would be to be home in Kamalant, to have a deep and refreshing bath, to put on clean clothes, and to order a meal to be served in her own apartment. The chef would tempt her appetite with salads, spicy meats, and sugared fruits and pastries.

The heat seemed even more unbearable than usual. Directly after lunch she went into the comparative coolness of the bed cave and lay down on the fur-covered slab. She loosened the rope girdle of her gown and daydreamed about fountains and cool shadowy pools until she fell asleep.

When she woke her forehead was wet and pools of sweat had collected in the hollows of her collarbone. She sat up slowly, her head swimming. The old aunt on the farther bed shelf snored. Her wrinkled old skin showed no sign of the oppressive heat. Her hands were folded placidly over her stomach.

Antia slipped quietly through the front room, where others drowsed away the hot afternoon. Outside the sun hit her like a white sword. For a moment she could see nothing at all. Then, through a kind of greenish haze, she saw Jodril. He was standing quite still under her favorite tree. Looking at something in his hand. Not just looking, but reading intently, so intently that he never heard her approach.

"Hey, that's my diary. Give it to me!"

He started, flushed, then deliberately turned his back on her and went on reading.

"It's mine. You have no right to . . . "

"You had no right to put down stuff like this."

"My private thoughts. For me alone . . . "

"Then who is this Eskoril?"

"Jealous?" The word just slipped out and she wished it unsaid.

He looked at her with contempt and then fended her off with one arm while he deliberately tore out the pages she had written that morning. Then he tossed the book at her feet and tore the loose sheets into tiny scraps. He let the wind scatter them over the brick pavement.

"Oh, how dare you!" She stamped her foot.

"How dare you write such things about Roshan. All those questions . . . what are you, a spy? Is that why you came here?"

She flushed. "I came because your father invited me, remember? And I've written nothing that was not true. If you have anything to hide it must be bad. Perhaps you are plotting against Kamalant. You're probably jealous of everything we have that you do not."

He laughed. "Of *Kamalant*?"

Her rage had nothing to spend itself against in the face of his icy contempt. "And if I want to climb that stupid dune I will. I'm going now in fact and you're not going to stop me."

"Oh, no you don't." He caught her wrist.

"Let her go." Shudi had come out without either of them noticing. "Let her go, Jodril. Only if she is destined for the truth will she be able to see it."

Was *that* what Shudi had said? What did it mean?

# 5

Antia hitched up her white desert robe and set out to climb the Great Dune. This time she tackled the slope at an angle, avoiding the steepest places where the wind had worn the surface into deep scallops. Her anger bore her up until she was almost at the summit. By then her knees were trembling and her calf muscles were so painfully cramped that she sank to the sand. I can't go on, she thought, drawing in deep gasps of hot, dry air. Not another step.

She looked back. From this height the village was a pattern of dark squares set out like a castles board on the desert floor, and the oasis was a small greenish stain on the overwhelming tan of the desert. "Destined for the truth." She groaned and forced herself to her feet. Left foot down. Right foot up and forward. And again. She began to count. Four, five . . . twenty-four, twenty-five . . . forty-seven, forty-eight . . .

There. She had made it! Now she would find out this great secret of Roshan. She looked eagerly around. The dune stretched to leeward in a gentle curve down toward a narrow valley, beyond which rose a battlement of red cliff, raw rock breaking through the gentle yellow-brown of the sand like a wound. Around and beyond the cliffs was a tumble of rocks and beyond that again, fading into the dancing heat, was the illimitable desert.

To left and right, wind-scalloped and sharpened, ran the crest of the dune. On and on. How silent it was. Nothing but the hammer of her heart and the gasping noise of her lungs.

The sun, dropping rapidly in the western sky, caught in its gleam a strange carved pillar that stood solitary at the foot of the cliff, like a marker. Its shadow ran along the ground and caressed the base of the cliff. Antia was reminded of the carved sundial in the middle of the rose garden at the palace in Malan.

A sudden breeze flattened her robe against her body. For an instant she remembered the scent of roses and her last meeting with Eskoril. Then the moment was gone and the hot breeze carried nothing but a faint scent of zaramint, and the smell of hot rock and sand. And something else . . . she did not know what. The wild scent of the desert perhaps. It spoke of all that the desert was. Lonely and proud. Stark and beautiful. Harsh and loving. Now she understood how Lady Sofi had felt.

As the sun fell toward the western horizon the wind strengthened. It lifted sand from the crest of the dune and blew it away in smoke. Antia stared to the horizon and seemed to see, as if she were on an eagle's wings, the curve of the planet. The dry wind ceaselessly scoured it, purifying it. She shivered and shut her eyes against the sight. How far would the wind blow before it met an obstacle as great as this dune? How many days' ride would it be to the next mountain? Or to the great ocean that circled Roshan? How huge, how empty was this planet that turned beneath her, moving through the heavens in the elaborate dance of the sky gods.

Who was she, Princess Antia, heir to the throne of Kamalant and Komilant? What was she, with her chests full of clothes, her caskets of jewels?

"I am nothing," she said aloud. "I am worth nothing at all." She fell to her knees with her hands over her face.

The sand whispered around her. She leaned forward and traced her name on the crest of the dune. *Antia, daughter of Prince Naiman of Kamalant and Komilant.*

The wind lifted the sand and blew it along the leeward slope. The words smudged and vanished. The sand was smooth again.

"Now I am nothing," she said aloud. But she no longer felt sad. It was more as if she were free of all the weight of ownership, the clutter of her possessions. Even her anger with Jodril, her unsure love for Eskoril, were suddenly not important anymore. "Why, I am free!"

When she got to her feet she saw that the shadow of the curving dune had blotted out the valley with its strange carved pillar. Now nothing lay between her and the rosy crest of the ridge opposite but a lake of shadow. She turned to go back to the village . . . and screamed.

Between her and the sun stood a dark shadow. Then it moved and she saw that it was a very old person, shorter than she was, covered with a hooded gown of tan homespun. Antia had seen Shudi weaving stuff just like it on a loom set up in the courtyard of her house. She peered through the shadows of the hood, wondering if it were one of the aunts or uncles sent to fetch her. She could see nothing but the gleam of two eyes.

"Who are you?" It came abruptly, almost rudely, but she was still shaken by the sudden appearance.

"I am Sandwriter." The voice was deep with age, but definitely that of a woman. "I welcome you to my Roshan, daughter."

"To your. . . ?" Antia couldn't help smiling. The air of authority was such a strange contrast to the ragged gown.

"Yes, to my Roshan. The real one. You entered it when you wrote your name in the sand. You are one of us now. You are of the sand."

"But I . . . "

69

"You have written and the wind has taken your name. It is done."

"But I am not even a Roshanite. I am a visitor from Kamalant."

"I know who you are, Princess."

"How...? Oh, of course, you saw me write my name. That is it, isn't it?" Antia tried to laugh.

The eyes did not move from her face. "We have met before, Princess, in your hour of need. We will meet again, the wind tells me, in the hour of Roshan's need. Until then, good-bye."

Two skinny hands shot out from the bundled robe to catch Antia's arms. She was turned until she faced south. Then a sharp push between the shoulder blades caught her off balance so that she had to run to stop pitching headlong. Running and sliding, she was halfway down the steep slope before she was able to slow down, to skid to a stop, to look back.

The crest of the dune was a wavering line against the sky. There was no sound but the dry sighing of the wind over the sand and the flutter of her robe about her ankles. Where had the old woman gone to? Where indeed had she come from? Was she from the village? Had they been playing some elaborate game with her?

At the bottom she looked back again. The dune lay like a sleeping beast, its crest and western slope bathed in rosy light, the rest carved out of shadow. Soon it would be quite dark. Supper would be ready. She should go before they began to worry about her. Slowly she walked back to the village, stopping now and then to look back. It was as if she didn't want to leave.

What had actually happened to make her feel so different? She felt as if she had been made the present of a great secret, only to find that it made no sense. She longed to talk to someone, but who was there? Jodril would laugh. It was too difficult to make Shudi understand. Better to keep the secret to herself. Once back in Lohat she would write to Eskoril and tell him everything that had happened on this strange journey across the desert of Roshan. Eskoril was wise. He would explain it to her.

But there would be no harm in asking a few innocent questions of Jodril and Shudi, to see their reaction. That was what Eskoril would wish her to do, she reminded herself. Then she felt a sudden shiver of distaste, like biting on a sour chepa. To lie, even to act a lie, was a very long way from the truth she had felt at the top of the dune. But that was only a dream, or something very like it, she told herself briskly. *This* is the reality. The secret of Roshan and my mission for Eskoril.

So as soon as she got back to the courtyard, she smiled at Jodril, who was sitting talking with Shudi and Atmon. "That was a good view, though I don't know why you made all that fuss, Jodril. I suppose it is the cliff on the north side that has stopped the Great Dune from traveling as the others have done, and that is why it is so big."

"Did you explore the cliff?" Shudi stopped spinning to ask her. She noticed that Atmon's busy hands were also stilled.

"No, I didn't. The view from the top was spectacular enough. What a climb."

Shudi's spindle twirled again and Atmon shaved another sliver off the tent peg he was whittling. The cliff, she thought. That is the secret. She wondered why her cleverness did not make her feel as pleased with herself as once it would.

"I *was* curious about that strange carved pillar at the base of the cliff. It looked as if it had been placed there on purpose."

Shudi's spindle rolled across the courtyard and Jodril jumped up to retrieve it.

"Not on purpose." Atmon spoke slowly, so that in spite of his thick accent she could understand him. "They are called handars, these pillars. They are made of soft rock, you understand, and the wind carves them."

71

"The wind?"

"Yes. It is so."

"Clever wind," said Antia lightly, and again felt a shiver run between Shudi and Atmon, the desert dwellers. She suspected that Jodril knew little more than she did. The secret, whatever it was, was a desert secret.

On the seventh day the caravan returned from Monar, the kroklyns laden with dried fish and dates, the five drivers shamefaced. After saying farewell to Shudi and Atmon, the children, the uncles and the aunts, Antia and Jodril climbed on the back of their beast and set out toward the west.

Antia turned and looked back at the Great Dune. Its crest was a frozen wave, sharpened by the wind, sand blowing off it like spume. It would have been fitting if *she* had been there to see them leave, just as it would have been fitting if Eskoril had been at the port of Malan to wish her well on the start of her journey. But there was no one watching now, as there had been no one at Malan.

The four-day journey seemed to last forever. The drivers continued sulky and defensive. She guessed that they were afraid that Jodril might report them and that they would lose their jobs. As for Antia, she was polite to Jodril, but no more. Her whole mind was occupied with thinking about Sandwriter and wondering what she should tell Eskoril about that strange meeting. When she ignored Jodril or answered only in a pre-occupied manner, he turned away and began to be very busy helping to feed and water the other kroklyns as well as looking after his own beast.

"Aren't I good enough to feed my own beasts, then?" the chief driver challenged Jodril on the second night.

"It's not that. I like to keep busy."

"Your job is looking after the young lady, in't? You lost her

72

once this trek, din' you? Maybe you'd better pay her more heed. I'll look after my own beasts."

Antia found it hard not to laugh when she overheard this exchange, but the desert seemed to have left her with a sense of tolerance, and she forced her mouth into a stern line and pretended to be writing in her diary.

On the fourth day, in midafternoon, they saw the mirage of Lohat, floating upside down above the horizon like a city reflected in a lake. Two hours later their kroklyn began to twitch. Its stride lengthened. Antia, who was holding the reins, felt the muscles of its sides and saw the neck stretch out, the small head weaving from side to side so that she could see the flash of its eyes.

Within another hour the flat roofs were visible above the encircling mud brick wall. Their kroklyn was in the lead. This is fun, thought Antia, like horse racing. In the events at Malan she had always been a winner.

"Give me the reins," Jodril shouted in her ear. "Keep low and hang onto the saddle. You're losing control."

"Nonsense!" Antia clung to the beast with thighs and knees and toes. She grasped the reins tightly. "Come on, then, you hairy monster," she shouted. "We'll beat the others to Lohat, won't we?"

The kroklyn rolled back its eyes and stretched its long neck out even further. Its stride lengthened. They were far ahead of the rest of the caravan. She heard the chief driver call a warning in a hoarse voice and she spared a hand to wave gaily back, before grabbing the rein again. The loaded panniers beneath the double saddle thumped against the beast's hairy sides.

Jodril yelled at her. She could feel his arms on either side of her trying to reach past her and grab the reins. "Don't you dare," she screamed back. "I had the reins this morning and I'm in charge."

She leaned forward, her taut muscles aching at the pull of

73

the reins. These creatures were incredibly powerful. The wind of their passing tore away her headcovering so that her black hair, which she had carelessly bundled into a net, fell loose and flew out behind her, whipping Jodril across the face. It didn't matter. Nothing mattered. The speed was wonderful. She was riding faster than the wind, faster than life. If she could only ride like this forever she would be able to forget all the things that had been worrying her since . . . since, Sandwriter.

"Give me the reins, stupid," Jodril yelled again, batting hair out of his eyes. "The drivers were right. You're nothing but trouble and bad luck. Look out, we're almost at the gate!"

Antia looked up at the changed tone, to see the curved archway dead ahead. She hauled back desperately at the reins and felt them cut the soft palms of her hands. If only I'd brought gloves, she thought. The kroklyn strode on, neck and tail outstretched.

"Whoa, there! Easy! Oh, what *do* you say to a kroklyn?"

They crossed the shadow of the gate's arch, and a stride later were beneath the arch itself. Antia hauled on the reins with every last bit of her strength and the kroklyn broke stride and slowed to what, in a horse, would be a smart gallop. Clinging to the saddle behind her, Jodril yelled warnings. A blur of people scattered to right and left. They were passing stalls piled with fruit. There was a crash and an angry voice. Then they were through the market and running uphill.

Now at last the kroklyn began to slow down. Ahead was a wall with a low arch set in it. Antia ducked quickly and felt masonry brush her shoulders. The kroklyn stopped so abruptly that she pitched forward against the saddle horn. She could feel its sides heave. Two men ran to its head, forcing it to kneel, and as soon as it was down, she swung her leg out of the saddle and slid down past the pannier to the ground. Her knees were trembling and she grabbed the pannier for support.

"That was fun!" She hoped he wouldn't hear her voice wobble.

"Fun? You idiot! You moron! You could have killed someone. Did you see what you did to that date stall?"

"Oh dear. I did hear something, but it was all happening so fast. Never mind. See that the bill for the damage is sent to me. I won't argue with it. . . ."

"You really think money'll do anything, don't you? Suppose one of the children had been killed? How much is a child worth in Kamalant?"

She turned, her face white. "No one was hurt or . . . or anything, were they, Jodril? I didn't mean . . . it was just a joke."

"It's only luck that no one was. But what about the kroklyn? You've half killed him, riding like that."

She looked up anxiously. The kroklyn lifted its wedge-shaped head from its water pail and looked back at her. It lifted its lip in what she could swear was a smile, showing its green teeth. Its eye gleamed wickedly. It blew a bubble at her and went on drinking.

The color came back to Antia's cheeks. "Nonsense, Jodril," she said briskly. "The kroklyn had a great run and enjoyed it thoroughly. So did I. So stop trying to spoil it all and let's go home."

"Maybe you did, but I certainly didn't. Riding behind a madwoman. Eating your hair. Look at you now . . . just like a tramp."

"Pooh!" She tucked her hair under her headcovering. Then she walked out of the stables.

"Where do you think you're going?"

She turned in the shadow of the arch. "Home."

"You don't know the way."

She didn't bother to answer, but stepped out into the brilliant light, shading her eyes with her hand. She was in an unfamiliar part of Lohat. To her left a cloud of dust and the hoarse cries of the drivers warned her that the rest of the caravan would be upon her in a moment. She turned to the right and began to walk rapidly away. She turned right at the next crossroads and slowed down to look about her.

There was a walled well at the end of the street and she sat down composedly on the stone steps around it. It wasn't long before a small girl appeared, barefooted and dusty, sucking a juicy fig and staring at the stranger with brilliant blue eyes. Antia beckoned her and she came over shyly.

"Do you know the house of Chief Hamrab?"

"Who does not?" The accent was thick, but the nod was clear in any language.

"Will you show me the way? I will give you a piece of silver."

"Silver? What for?"

"You could buy many figs, all you want to eat, and maybe a pair of shoes."

The child laughed. "The figs are from my father's tree. As for shoes, who needs them? They slip on the cobbles."

This was true, Antia found, as she tried to keep up with her small guide, who walked rapidly through the twisting back alleys of the town until Antia began to think that she did not know the way after all. Then, quite unexpectedly, they were on the main street, just one house away from home.

"Wait. I will ask the doorman for some money." Antia remembered that all her belongings were still in the pannier back at the stable. She hoped that Jodril would think to bring them.

The child shook her head and finished her fig.

"But you must have something." Antia slipped one of the silver bangles from her left wrist and put it on the child's arm. "There now. Take care of it and you can tell your friends it once belonged to a princess."

The little girl danced out of sight into the network of alleys, her arm held out admiringly in front of her. Antia knocked at the door and, when Thadron opened it, walked thankfully into the darkness of the hall. Whatever happens, she thought, whether the roof should fall in or the house catch fire, I am going to have a *bath*!

"Nan, Nan, where are you?" She crossed the hall with its smelly oil lamp and pushed aside the bead curtain to her room. "Oh, Nan. Get me a bath at once, I beg you!"

"Hmm? What, what? Oh, Princess, dear, you are back! I was sleeping. But what has happened to you? You look terrible. I know what it is, you need a bath. Now don't argue with me, my love. Just get out of those terrible clothes while I order a bath."

She bustled out, clapping her hands and shouting for servants. Antia laughed weakly and fell back on one of the beds. She shut her eyes.

"Come, precious, sit up, do. Let me help you out of those clothes. Oh, gracious, look at your hair! Come, my sweet, I can't lift you. Into the tub. See, I have put in your best bath oil. Climb in and you will soon feel better."

Antia climbed wearily into the small tin tub. She sank into the water with a groan. "Oh, I have dreamed of this for over a ten-day, Nan."

She sat back with her eyes shut and let Nan wash her, until a too firm swipe with the cloth jolted her out of her lethargy. "Ouch! Oh, careful, Nan, that hurt!"

"What is it? Oh, my precious, your hands! What have you done to your beautiful hands!"

"Hush, Nan, you'll have everyone running in here thinking I've been murdered. Just don't scrub so hard."

"But they're bleeding. We must have a doctor. I suppose they do have doctors in this benighted place?"

"No, Nan, don't fuss. Your salves are better than any doctor's. And you are to say nothing, do you understand?"

"Yes, my pet, if you say so. But what caused these terrible cuts?"

Antia giggled in spite of the pain. "The kroklyn's reins. It was my own fault, Nan. I had no gloves."

"You were driving those horrid beasts? What was Jodril thinking about to . . . "

"It was a game, Nan. Now stop fussing. My hands will heal. But my hair . . . are you ever going to be able to wash the sand out of it?"

By the time Antia had been wrapped in the thick soft towels that Nan had brought from Kamalant, she was more than half asleep. She didn't notice that the dress Nan had picked for her was quite one of the most elaborate, a gown of pale green embroidered all over with the tiny mauve flowers of the *hamla* bush. She only roused herself as Nan tied the sash.

"Oh, Nan, how could you?"

"About time you looked pretty for the young man," Nan muttered unrepentedly.

"I've a good mind to . . . " But then the gong went for dinner and there was no time. Antia looked in dismay at her red, swollen hands.

"Just put some of the salve on my palms and find me the green lace mittens. Hurry, Nan. I mustn't be late."

The mittens were long, reaching to her elbows and leaving her fingers uncovered. Antia stretched out her hands and looked at them. "That will do very well. They're ridiculously formal for Lohat, but I cannot go to dinner covered in bandages."

She kissed Nan's cheek and hurried out into the hall to find that the candles had all been lit and the table decorated as if for a feast. Chief Hamrab and Lady Sofi were already there, and Jodril hovered in the background. His blond hair was damp from the bath, like the feathers of a newly hatched eagle. His expression was uneasy.

Antia dropped a curtsey to her hosts. "I am sorry to have kept you waiting. Nan does fuss so and she couldn't get the sand out of my hair."

Lady Sofi smiled. "I must show you how to braid it so tightly that the sand cannot get into it before you go on another desert crossing."

Antia breathed a sigh of relief. So nothing had been said about her getting lost in the sandstorm or of her wild ride into the city. The meal was served and she found herself enjoying the dish of plainly cooked vegetables that was set in front of her.

"Your trip has certainly improved your color! You were so pale when you first arrived."

Antia smiled politely but said nothing. They would never understand that in Kamalant a white skin and soft hands were a sign of wealth and power. Nan had already had fits over the sunburn on her nose and the threat of freckles across her cheekbones.

"Was your tour interesting?" Chief Hamrab asked.

"Yes, thank you. Most interesting."

"What were your impressions of Monar?"

She shot an agonized glance at Jodril, who sat opposite her. Had he said nothing at all of their adventures? Perhaps he didn't want to get the kroklyn drivers into trouble. His face told her nothing, though his cheeks were flushed.

"It was interesting, too," she said cautiously. "But I am glad to be back."

"I thought you would have enjoyed the swimming. The beaches are so much nicer," Lady Sofi said reproachfully.

"It was pleasant."

"And what about the dance group. . . ?"

This was beyond her. She looked desperately at Jodril and

79

this time he stammered. "Oh, the . . . the group was rehearsing a new act or something. There was nothing to see." His face was scarlet.

"What a shame. How strange. I was sure . . ."

"The oases were most fascinating." Antia tried to fill the awkward gap. "Especially the one by the big dune."

"Did you have time to visit the village?"

"Yes. Remarkable. I've never seen anything like it."

Luckily, then, the single servant returned with a second course, something special, judging by the exclamations. Antia found that it was gazelle, cooked in a sauce of pomegranates. She began to cut the slices on her plate, and sweat broke out on her forehead at the pain in her hands. She pretended to eat until the others had finished, and then motioned the servant to remove her plate also.

She caught Jodril by the sleeve as his parents left the hall. "I could kill you!" she hissed.

"What did I do?"

"You could have warned me that you hadn't told them anything about the storm or us being left at the oasis."

"Well, there really wasn't much time. Anyway, if you're so bright you can survive a sandstorm and handle a homing kroklyn, not to mention getting home from the stables by yourself, you should have been able to handle it with a few cues."

"What cues? You were no help at all. What do I think of Monar? What about the dancers? Lucky for you I didn't give the whole thing away."

"Lucky for me? You were the one who ran off. You're . . ."

"You were supposed to be there to look after me. Anyway, I'm the guest. What could they do to me?"

"Send you home."

"Well, I'm surprised you didn't tell them all the terrible

80

things I did, then, so you could be rid of me. As if I'd care. Oh, for running water and properly cooked food!"

"You really made that clear, didn't you? Dressed like a wedding cake and picking at the food. You really showed Mother what you think of her household."

"I didn't mean . . . it wasn't like that . . . "

"Just don't treat her like that again or . . . "

"Or what?"

"I'll . . . " He grabbed her hands. She cried out and went white. "What's the matter? Are you ill?"

"It's nothing. Please let me go."

He turned her hands over. She curled her fingers over the palms but he forced them straight. "There's blood on these gloves. Your hands!"

She gave a shaky laugh. "It was the reins. I do have riding gloves. I just didn't think to bring them with me to Roshan. Silly of me."

"The doctor should see them."

"No. Hush, don't talk so loudly. Why do you think I wore these ridiculous mittens? Nan has looked after them. I'll be all right." She pulled her hands away. "I don't know about you, but I'm exhausted. Good night, Jodril."

It was two days before the swelling in her palms had gone down enough for her to write to Eskoril. She told him every detail of the sandstorm, of how she was lost and then found herself in the village.

*It sounds incredible, but I know I am remembering true. There was a person in that cave with me. Someone saved me and bathed me in the pool. Some of the other things make no sense, like seeing fire on the water – I expect I was delirious with heat and thirst. But I do know that I was in the cave and then was taken to the village underground.*

81

She bit the top of her pen. "You must tell me everything," Eskoril had said. "You do not know enough of statecraft, Princess, to discern what is important to me." He had smiled, to take the sting from his words, and her heart had flip-flopped in her chest, out there in the fragrant rose garden.

Now, looking back, she wondered. Why had he been so rude? He was her tutor and he knew how advanced she was in the languages of Rokam, in mathematics and science, in history and statecraft. She was as capable of knowing what was important as he. So in the end she did *not* tell him about her race back to Lohat; it was a somewhat undignified escapade for a princess. Nor did she mention her meeting with Sandwriter. There was something special and private about that, something she could not share even with her most dear Eskoril.

She signed the letter, blotted it, sealed it with her seal, and tucked it into the front of her dress. It wanted a half hour till lunch, which was an informal meal anyway. Nan was busy in the servants' quarters. The house was quiet. She slipped quietly from her room and crossed the dark hall like a shadow.

The blaze of heat and light beyond the front door made her gasp. As she blinked, she saw a shadow move by the arch. She had forgotten the gatekeeper. Oh, well, he was old and would not be a bother to her. She walked boldly across the courtyard and motioned for him to open the gate. "I will be back in a short while . . . " What was his name? Thadron, that was it. "I have a small errand, Thadron, so watch for my return."

"Nobody goes out at noon, miss." His creaky voice was disapproving. "Allow me to do your errand."

"No. No, thank you." She walked quickly through the gate he held reluctantly ajar. She bit her lip. Now I have made myself conspicuous just when I wanted to be most secret. I should have waited till evening. But then there would be so many people about.

She walked slowly down the hill to the market. How quiet it was! Every door and shutter was closed against the burning heat. The only sound was that of her sandals clattering over the cobbles.

The marketplace drowsed. How stupid of her! Would she even be able to find the stall of the saddlemaker, Berron, with no one to ask? The tables were deserted, the pierced walls looked blank, though perhaps there were eyes peering through the holes at the crazy foreigner.

She came to the last stall and hesitated. Then she knocked on the rough wooden door behind it. There was a shuffling sound and the door opened a crack. "You are Berron, the saddlemaker?"

It opened wider. "And if I am?"

"I am to give you this letter."

He took it with a hand that left a grimy fingerprint on the fold of crisp paper. He stared at the superscription so long that she wondered if indeed he could read.

"Oh, ah!" he said at last and closed one eye and laid his finger along the side of his nose. "I'll see it gets to the pretty gentleman, that I will."

Blushing furiously, Antia fled. She didn't look back until she reached the corner. She leaned against the wall, panting, and thought she saw a shadow dart across the patch of bright sunlight at the other end. She blinked and there was nothing, not a dog nor a bird.

She wiped her face with the corner of her scarf and set off uphill. By the time she had reached the great door her head was pounding and she felt a little sick.

Old Thadron shook his head. "Not at midday. The sun is our life, but it is also our death. Remember and take care, little miss."

She pressed a coin into his hand, hoping that it would shut his mouth. Then she stumbled back to her own room. Thank goodness Nan had not returned. She could not face questions or the thought of lunch. She pulled off her dress and lay on the bed in her undershift.

Take care . . . Thadron's words drifted through her head. Take care. Everyone in Lohat slept during the heat of noon. Everyone but herself and that shadow at the bottom of the marketplace. Who could it have been? She slipped into a fever-ish dream in which she was lost in the alleys of Lohat with something mysterious and terrifying stalking her.

Later, she began to wonder who would collect the letter she had left for Eskoril. Why would he not allow it to be sent by fast steamship, as her dutiful letters to Uncle Rangor and Aunt Sankath were sent? It was very strange. She began to feel uneasy, and when, four days later, she found a letter tucked beneath her pillow she turned on Nan.

"Nan, where did this come from? You must know."

"On my honor, precious, I do not. It is a love note from Jodril, I'll be bound. I expect one of the servants slipped it in." She cackled at her own wit. Antia turned her back and took the letter over to the window. It was even more terse than Eskoril's last.

*It is imperative that you find the person who took you to the village. He holds the secret of the Source. This is what I seek. You must find the person and notify me. I will get the truth from him. Make haste.*

She stared blankly at the paper. The Source. What did he mean? *You must find the person . . . I will get the truth from him. . . .* She shivered suddenly and crumpled the sheet of paper in her hand. If a Roshante did not choose to share a secret, especially a secret of the desert, nothing would make him break silence. She was sure of that. What had Eskoril in mind?

She gulped and bit her knuckles to hold back the tears. Tears were a waste of time. What she needed was a clear head. *This is what I seek*, Eskoril had written. *I will get the truth* . . . It did not sound like Eskoril, her quiet tutor. This letter sounded more like . . . well, more like Aunt Sankath. Imperious. Demanding.

Oh, what have I done? And what can I do to put things right when I don't understand what is going on?

# 6

"If you don't want to go, all you have to do is say so, Antia."

"What?" She tore her mind back from its ever-present worries about Eskoril. "I'm sorry. I didn't . . . Go where, Jodril?"

"Swimming. There's a pleasant beach south of Lohat with a reef that discourages the sea serpents. We could go early while it's still cool and take a picnic."

"That would be nice. I'd like that." It would be good to get away, not just from the heat of the low port city, but from her thoughts. From that nagging feeling that she had done something dreadfully wrong in telling Eskoril about the Great Dune and the cave.

They set out shortly after sunrise in a small covered cart pulled by a shaggy gray lema, and for an hour traveled along a twisting cliff-top road that gave them breathtaking views of the ocean, sometimes almost beneath the wheels of the cart.

"But don't worry," said Jodril cheerfully. "These lemas are more surefooted than they look."

At last the land dipped and a hairpin track took them down the cliff to a tiny bay, cut off from the rest of the coast by a fall of rocks at either end. A wrack of timber and dried seaweed marked the high tide line, and rock pools held all sorts of strange creatures and festoons of purple and blue seaweed. Beyond the rocks the sand glistened, smoothed by the out-going tide.

"Shall we swim before it gets too hot? You can change in the cart."

Antia agreed and climbed out of the robe she had borrowed from Lady Sofi and into a bathing dress, also Lady Sofi's. She felt ridiculous in knee-length cotton trousers and short tunic. Would Jodril laugh? But when she climbed shyly out of the cart it was to see him in a similar outfit.

He helped her over the sharp rocks, obviously on his best behavior today. His hand was comfortingly warm and strong, but once on the sand she pulled hers away. "Race you into the water!"

The sea foamed around her ankles, her knees. She dived into a wave and swam with strong, crisp strokes. When at last she turned to look back she was almost at the limit of the bay and the cart was a small white dot on the shore. The water was cool and the air still fresh. She dived under and came up, blinking the saltiness from her eyes. Her worries seemed to fall from her shoulders and dissolve. She swam a leisurely course back to shore.

"Oh, that was wonderful!"

"We can come as often as you like."

"Every day, then!" She laughed and shook out her hair.

They played *diska* until their bathing suits were dry, and then Jodril said they should rest in the shade. "We can swim again later, if you like."

"Could we eat now, I'm starving!"

Jodril spread the contents of the food box on a cloth in the shade of the cart, and they squatted on either side of it.

"Would you like to go kroklyn riding, once your hands are healed," he asked suddenly, when they had got over the worst of their hunger.

"I should love to. And they're healed already. See." She held out her hands, palms up. He took one of them in his and traced the pink scars with a finger. "I wouldn't have had that happen for anything."

She blushed and pulled her hand away. "It was my fault. It was stupid of me not to remember my gloves. Jodril, I wanted to say something . . . just . . . well, thank you for not giving me away to your father. But you never told me how much you had to pay the date merchant – the one whose stall I knocked over."

"There's nothing."

"I can't believe that."

He laughed. "Truly. I explained that you were a visitor and a girl and headstrong . . . "

"You lema! What did he say to that?"

Jodril flushed under his tan. "He just made a joke. But he wouldn't let me pay him anything."

"And you're not going to tell me the joke?"

"No!"

"Oh." She caught his eye, blushed, and then began to laugh too.

The sun's heat lay across Roshan like a weight. Jodril fell asleep in the small shade beneath the cart, but Antia's worries came creeping back and she couldn't relax. She stared at the waves rolling in toward the shore, rolling in from Kamalant and Komilant. Beyond that ocean was Eskoril.

It's the distance between us, she thought. When he was face-to-face with me in the rose garden it all made sense. Letters can be so confusing. They give the wrong impression. I have to trust him, that's all.

She looked down at Jodril, at the hawklike face, so like his father's, but unlined, golden brown, flushed with sleep. Her heart suddenly fluttered. That's stupid, she told herself firmly. He's only a boy. Eskoril is a man and so wise and good. But

. . . A sad dissatisfaction stirred within her, whether with Eskoril so far away or Jodril close beside her, she couldn't say. Oh, it's all such a muddle. She sighed and longed for it to get cooler and for Jodril to waken.

In the late afternoon they explored the rock pools and swam again, and laughed a great deal about very little. Antia forgot her worries until they were in the cart driving back to Lohat. Then they returned, heavier than ever because of the hours of happiness before.

Jodril stopped the cart at the top of the rise from which they could see the whole city below them, encircled by its wall of baked brick. "It's just like a map, isn't it? Look, Antia, you can see the kroklyn stables over to the right. And there's the market. Can you pick out our house?"

"No." Tears had sprung suddenly into her eyes and she turned her head away so he shouldn't see.

"What's the matter?"

"Nothing. I don't know what you mean."

"Of course you do. Antia, what is it? You're like two different people. One is full of fun and so nice to be with. The other is sulky and silent."

She bit her lip, longing to tell him everything, but not daring.

He sighed. "Why don't you tell me what's wrong? Isn't that what friends are for, to help?"

She stared out to sea, blinking, unable to say a word. After a while Jodril picked up the reins and urged the lema down the long slope to the city. When he stopped at the house gate, Antia jumped down. "Jodril, I'm sorry. I'd like your help but . . . but I can't. It was a lovely day. Thank you."

She ran into the house and cried bitterly until Nan came in to dress her for dinner. "Quarreling with your young man, is that it? Don't worry, my pet. It'll pass like summer rain, I promise you. And he's a dear boy. A lovely boy."

89

Nan was hopeless. Nan would never understand.

She reread Eskoril's letter before going to bed that night. It was falling to pieces from the many times she had read it and folded it small and hidden it away. She knew she shouldn't keep it, that Eskoril would trust her to have destroyed it, but she couldn't. If only she knew . . . who was the *real* Eskoril? The dear tutor of her childhood in Malan, or the arrogant man in this letter? She lay through the long night listening to Nan's snores.

"I thought we might hire a couple of kroklyns and go north up the coast," Jodril said at breakfast. "But you look tired. Maybe you would rather rest."

"No, let's get out. I can't stand being cooped up in here. If Lady Sofi can lend me riding gloves . . . "

Once out of the city she let her kroklyn have its head. The beast was in a playful mood, sensing that this was a day off rather than the hard slog of a laden caravan. It whipped its head from side to side, grinning at her evilly with its greenish teeth.

"Come on, then," she told it. "Let's go!" And it stretched out its snakelike neck and strode along the stony road. The wind flattened her robe against her body and the fresh sea air cleared her head. Little by little the weight of worry dropped away. She shook the reins and her nimble-footed kroklyn picked up speed.

When she finally slowed down, hot and out of breath, Jodril wasn't even in sight. She forced the kroklyn to kneel so that she could dismount. Here the road skirted a high cliff. The sea far below was like a piece of crushed fabric. Only the lacy line of foam at its edge was a reminder of the power of its waves and the restlessness of the tides. So deceptive, she thought idly. Then . . . I must test Eskoril. Find out what is really in his mind. Only then will I know what to do.

*Revered tutor*, she wrote in the quiet time before Nan came in to dress her for dinner. *I have a confession to make. Life is much less extraordinary than I made out in my letters. In fact it is so dull that I got a little carried away in the description I wrote you of my adventures. Forgive me, dear Eskoril, and consider my letters, as you originally suggested they should be, to be exercises in composition.*

*The more I consider how I exaggerated my adventures near the Great Dune, the more ashamed I am. In truth I was lost and was rescued by the people of the sand village of Ahman. But what came between was little more than a memory of feverish dreams. I should have waited longer before writing to you, and my last letter would have been more reasonable.*

*I have been in good health since my return to Lohat. Jodril and I have been ocean swimming and kroklyn riding. . . .*

Antia bit the top of her pen, reread what she had written and then quickly scrawled her signature, folded the paper and sealed it before she could change her mind. She would slip out of the house after supper and take it to the saddlemaker. Then she would have to be patient and wait for Eskoril's response.

It had been four days between leaving the last letter and receiving a reply. That was an incredibly short space of time for a letter to go from Roshan to Kamalant and return. Whoever picked up her letter must be using carrier birds. Four days. How could she bear to wait for four days?

But it was only on the second day, as she lay down for her noon siesta, that she heard something crackle beneath her pillow. Her hand slipped under and her fingers felt the small paper oblong. Her heart pounded. How had it got there? Who could be the carrier?

"Nan, who comes into this room?"

"No one but myself, pet. I don't want those strange servants poking among our things. I clean and dust myself. And

91

if I need help, like in moving a chest, then I ask for it and I stand right there watching till they take themselves off again."

"Yes. But I suppose anyone could just walk in when you are away. There are no locks anywhere, except on the front gate."

"That's true, my pet. And a funny way to live it is, if you ask me. But if I did catch a servant snooping I'd make such a fuss . . . oh, Lordy, is something missing?" She turned in the doorway.

"No, nothing like that," Antia said hastily. "I just wondered." She turned on her side and shut her eyes, waiting for the jangle of the curtain that would tell her Nan had left.

When it came she waited for a minute and then sat up, pulled the letter from under her pillow, and broke the seal.

*Princess, you do me wrong.* The black spikes were even more emphatic than usual. *Why have you ceased to trust me? Have the Chief of Roshan and his wife been whispering untruths in your ears? And have you believed them, in spite of everything that lies between you and me?*

Antia's cheeks flamed. The words danced like summer flies on the page. She blinked and read on.

*But alas, the distance between us is so great that I must speak no more of this.*

What *did* he mean? The distance between Roshan and Kamalant? Or the distance between the heir to the throne of the twin continents and her tutor? As if that would ever matter, dear Eskoril. She smoothed the page and read on quickly.

*But you have been false to me. Tell me the truth, Princess. In the matter of the cave and what you saw there – who was the person who tended you? Where was the cave relative to the village? How far did you wander from where the drivers stopped in the storm to the place where you became lost? How far would you judge the distance from the cave to the village of Ahman and in which direction? You speak of two pools – think, Princess. Did the water have an unusual taste? Can you recall unusual smells? How far was the pool of fire from the place where you were bathed?*

*Princess, I must have facts, not ramblings of swims or kroklyn rides with the young Chief. Do you hope to make me jealous? Reply at once. If you cannot help me because of your faulty memory or because you have lost faith in our cause . . .*

Our cause. What does he mean by *our* cause? Frowning, Antia returned to the letter.

*. . . then I will have to send others to Ahman to make inquiries. Very rough men, Princess, who would hesitate at nothing to find out the truth for me. Write to me at once. I await your answer impatiently.*
*Your devoted tutor. I wish I were more.*
   *Eskoril*

She stared at the spiky writing. That could not be his signature. The whole letter must be a forgery. Eskoril would never have written her such a letter, such a mixture of arrogant threats and suggested love. Never!

She slipped out of bed and unlocked her writing desk, to compare the signature with that on the last letter. They were identical. She swallowed, but then a new hope revived her. Perhaps that letter was not from Eskoril either. But how could she prove it? She walked up and down the room biting her thumbnail.

Her books! There was a volume of poetry that Eskoril had given her for a previous birthday. She snatched it down and opened it at the title page.

*To my princess and pupil on her twelfth birthday,*
*From her devout tutor Eskoril*

The handwriting was identical. She shuddered and dropped book and letters to her bed. That Eskoril should write like that to *her*. Half threats, half flatteries, wholly horrible! What dreadful trouble had her infatuation with Eskoril got her into? Worse still, got Roshan into?

She sat on the edge of her bed, her head in her hands, and tried to think. The pool of water. The pool of fire. A taste and a smell. What did it all *mean*? And why were the answers so important to Eskoril? What *was* the secret of Roshan? And how could she possibly put things right when she didn't even know what she had done wrong?

"Awake already, my love?"

She started. "Yes, Nan." She slipped Eskoril's letters into the book of poetry. Across the room her desk stood unlocked. In a moment Nan's sharp eyes would notice and there would be questions. She thought quickly. "Nan, dear, would you ask one of the servants if Jodril is awake? Perhaps he has plans for us this afternoon."

Nan smiled approvingly and bustled from the room. In a flash Antia had laid the book back on the shelf and locked her writing desk. She was standing by the pierced wall when Nan returned.

"He asks if you would rather ride or walk, my pet?"

"Walk, I think. I will wear one of the robes Lady Sofi has lent me, and my strong sandals."

When she was ready to leave, she picked up the poetry book and said casually. "There is something I want to show Jodril."

Nan chuckled and quoted a country saying about lovers and poetry that made Antia blush up to her forehead. Honestly, Nan had but a single thought in her old head!

She still felt confused when she met Jodril, so that when he

94

suggested they walk down to the harbor she agreed, though she would rather he had picked a quieter place.

"May I carry your book?"

"No, thank you. I can slip it into the front of my gown, the cord will hold it."

"You wanted to show me something. . . ?"

"Yes. I . . . " She stopped. What could she tell Jodril? Perhaps it would be safer to say nothing at first, but to try to pry from him the significance of the Great Dune, which must surely be part of the secret of the cave and the pools. "Oh, let's just walk," she said at last.

There was a packet in from the Far Isles, which lay in the Great Ocean far to the east of Roshan. The harbor was crowded, and at any other time Antia would have found it entrancing to wander along the quay, listening to the strange accents, seeing the quaint costumes, and picking over the exotic wares that were spread out for sale. Only now the book, with Eskoril's letter in it, burned against her chest like a hot coal.

"Couldn't we go somewhere quieter?" she asked desperately.

"Honestly, Antia, I don't know what to make of you. I thought the ship would amuse you. Perhaps you would rather stroll in the Resting Place among the dead. It's quiet enough up there!"

She didn't even notice his sarcasm. "Yes, that would be nice."

He stared, then shrugged and led the way up a winding road out of the city to the graveyard, high on the hill southeast of Lohat. Behind it the silver meshes of the dew catchers shone in the sun. When early mists rolled in across the sea these nets caught the moisture for the thirsty people of Lohat. Right now the air was dry and the dew catchers hung empty.

But it was a peaceful place, surrounded by a low brick wall,

95

with only a few stunted thornbushes to cast a little shade. Antia sat on a stone bench and looked down past the bustling harbor to the quiet of the open sea. She sighed. Jodril leaned back and whistled under his breath.

"Do you have to do that?" she snapped.

"Shall I leave you alone? I'm sure you'll be able to find your way home, as you did from the stables the other day."

"No, don't go. I'm sorry. I want to talk to you. It's just . . . well . . . it's all so difficult . . . "

"I won't bite." His voice was kind again. He took her hand, smoothed over the pink scars on the palm with his thumb.

"Jodril, I've got to ask you something, something terribly important. More depends on the answer than you could begin to guess."

"Ask away, then."

"I'm not just prying. You must understand. I *have* to know. It's about . . . about the Great Dune. And the cave and the pools." His hand tightened on hers so abruptly that she cried out and pulled it away.

"You don't know what you're asking, Antia."

"I thought we were friends. Why do you want to keep things from me?" I sound like Eskoril, she thought distastefully.

"Because they're not just secrets, Antia. They are sacred to the desert dwellers. They are the heart and soul of Roshan. I can't . . . and even if I knew it all you'd not understand."

"Because I'm a foreigner? From Kamalant?"

"Because you are not of the desert."

"You know your father and my uncle were arranging a marriage between us? Well, wouldn't I have been part of Roshan then? Part of the desert?"

He shook his head. "It's not that simple."

She pressed on. "You know I saw a cave and two pools.

96

You read it in my diary and you tore up the pages, so I know it's important. But why? Why won't you tell me?"

"I can't."

"Perhaps it isn't important after all. Perhaps I dreamed the whole thing." She let her voice go flat and her shoulders sag, while she watched him from under her eyelids. She could see the lines about his mouth relax. "Well, if it's all in my mind it wouldn't really matter if I told someone else about it, someone who was not of Roshan. If it were just a dream . . ."

He caught her wrists. "You told someone?"

"I said *if* . . ." Her voice faded. How dark his eyes were, with the cold merciless stare of a hawk's.

"You told your nurse, perhaps? You told Nan." His hands relaxed their grip and she pulled hers away and rubbed her wrists.

"No, not Nan. I wrote to . . . to my tutor."

"Who is he?"

"His name is Eskoril. He is the son of a minor court official in my uncle's court."

"At the court of Kamalant! And what exactly did you tell him?"

"Everything I could remember about the Dune and the cave and the pools."

"Why are you telling me now? So I'll forgive you and you can feel better? Well, I'm sorry, Princess, but that I cannot do. I don't know enough to know what damage you may have done. Eskoril is his name? I think I have heard it before."

"I'm sorry. I was afraid . . . then I hoped that maybe I had done no harm, that it wasn't important. Oh, Jodril, what *am* I to do? I'm so afraid of what Eskoril will do next. Look." She took out the book and handed him Eskoril's letters.

He read them through in silence and then tossed them into her lap. "What a creature! Half threats and half promises of love. Is this the person you've been dreaming of? And I

97

thought – well, you're welcome to him. He's nothing but a common spy."

"But it's not like that, Jodril." In her eagerness to defend Eskoril out tumbled the whole secret scene in the rose garden. It had seemed so reasonable at the time, when Eskoril's dark eyes were mesmerizing her, his hands holding hers. His sense of urgency. The sultry scent of roses.

Now, high above Lohat, in the clear desert air, she saw the expression of disbelief and disgust on Jodril's face. She faltered and stopped.

"And you accepted my father's invitation into our home as a *spy*?"

She felt her cheeks grow hot. How loyal and unbending were these Roshanites. Against Jodril she felt flighty and good-for-nothing. "But it wasn't like that. It didn't seem . . . " She stumbled, remembering her feelings beneath the desert night sky. She dredged up a word out of her past. "It was statecraft."

"Statecraft? What is that but a powerful word to make you feel in the right? After you have betrayed the hospitality of our house – my own feelings."

Her heart skipped, as it had done when she had watched him sleeping on the beach. It was suddenly desperately important that Jodril should think well of her. Yet she must stand up for Eskoril, however strangely he was behaving, for the sake of all he meant to her . . . *had* meant to her?

"I'm sorry," she stammered. "I didn't see it that way – as a betrayal – honestly I didn't. I didn't know you then, we weren't friends . . . " Her voice trailed off into silence.

"You didn't even *feel* it was wrong? The corruption of Kamalant! Well, you've told me the truth at last, and that is good. I must tell my father, you do see that? He will probably send you home, and he will certainly warn your uncle about this self-serving scorpion in his court."

Poor Eskoril, thought Antia. How could he live away from the grandeur of the palace? It was his life. Power was his life. She bit her lip. Power. That was what Eskoril loved. How stupid she had been, how gullible.

She blinked back tears. "I do see that you must tell your father. But please, Jodril, be careful. It is clear from Eskoril's letter that he feels very close to gaining what he wants – oh, if only he had told me what it was! 'It would change his fortunes,' was all he said. What can it be? We know it has something to do with the Great Dune and the pools in the cave. Only what cave? Where is it? If I only understood what it was all about perhaps I could help right the wrong I have done."

"How could we ever trust *you* with the secret of Roshan?" It was not said in anger, but matter-of-factly. She flinched as if he had slapped her. She had a sudden vision of herself walking along a road, coming to a fork, and taking the wrong path. From the very first I was stupid, she thought savagely, stupid and self-centered.

But perhaps it was not too late. "There must be some way I can prove to you that I really want to help. I'll do anything. If I were a Roshanite how would you test my honor in a matter so important?"

"Upon the Great Dune."

"Well, let's go back there, then."

He shook his head. "You are not of the sand."

Antia stared at him. Memory stirred within her of something she had shared with no one, and sudden hope lifted the corners of her mouth. "Oh, yes, I am."

"Nonsense. You don't even know what it means."

"That's true. But nevertheless I am. I wrote my name on the top of the dune and *she* came, out of nowhere it seemed."

"She? Shudi, perhaps." He laughed uneasily.

"No, it was not Shudi. It was an ancient woman, dressed in ragged brown homespun. Her eyes were so beautiful."

99

He was standing over her, staring. "And she actually spoke to you?"

"Oh, yes."

His mouth dropped open. Then he swallowed. "I have never even seen her myself. The secrets are not mine. Only when I am of age will my father take me there. Yet she spoke to *you*."

"Yes, truly. And . . . oh, Jodril, how silly of me not to think of it before. . . . I think it was *she* who rescued me from the storm and took me into the cave."

"Come on, then." He pulled her hand.

"What is it? What are we going to do?"

"We're going back to Ahman to ask for her help. We will go to Sandwriter!"

# 7

Antia stared up at the desert sky. The stars shone with a cold brilliance. "Go to sleep," Jodril had said. "I'll wake you when it's time." But she couldn't sleep.

She shut her eyes against the accusing stars and remembered the last awful ten-days, from her private meeting with Chief Hamrab to her return to the oasis of Ahman.

"I can't face your father," she had pleaded with Jodril. "You tell him." But after a long talk, Jodril had come out of the Chief's private chamber and told Antia that his father wished to see her.

Chief Hamrab had been kinder to her than Jodril, but the authority in his grave face and piercing eyes made her tremble. How different he was from the fat, lazy King Rangor.

"You were not to know of the fragility of Roshan, or of the care with which we nurture her as she nurtures us. I am sad that our trust in you has been damaged, but Jodril has convinced me that you were only led astray."

The fact that Jodril had stood up for her before his father was almost her undoing. She took a deep breath and swallowed. "And may I help put things right, if it is possible?"

"We can but try." Was that a smile at the corner of his mouth? Surely not. There was certainly nothing to smile about. "Jodril will escort you back to Ahman in the hope that Sandwriter will counsel you. We are all in her hands. And of course you must promise never again to communicate with Eskoril about anything you may know of Roshan."

"Oh, I swear," she gasped.

"Your word will be enough," he said gravely. "I will arrange for you to accompany a caravan leaving for Monar in six days."

"Oh, can't we go sooner?"

"If I sent you with a special escort, I might as well proclaim your intentions from the housetops. No, the next caravan leaves in six days. We must all be patient."

"What about Eskoril's last letter? If I don't answer it, what will he think?"

"It is clear to me that he has his spies in the city, who watch everything you do. The speed with which your letters reached him makes me suspect that he, too, is closer than you may have guessed. For the next six days I want you to be very visible. Swim. Ride. Shop in the market. Jodril will accompany you everywhere. Oh, please lighten the glum expression, Princess Antia! I want you to give the impression of a lighthearted girl with nothing on her mind but the good time she is having, and . . . " His mouth twitched again. "And her escort."

Antia blushed crimson and did not know where to look. But she had to admit that the Chief was a very wise man. Nothing she could think of to tell Eskoril would be as likely to be believed as reports that she was having a wonderful time and forgetting all about the mission he had entrusted her with.

But it had been the most difficult six days of her life, and when at last she and Jodril left the city on their laden kroklyn, she found out that it had been as wearing for Jodril.

"Thank goodness that's over," he had remarked as they

passed under the shadow of the city gate. "Now for heaven's sake stop talking and laughing and let's have some peace and quiet."

Now she lay, every part of her body janglingly awake. When, at last, the expected touch came to her shoulder she jumped and had to stifle a cry. At last!

She slipped from under her blanket and followed the shadowy figure to where their kroklyn lay sleeping. Jodril woke it with a brisk tap behind the ear and stopped its snarl with a stick of sweetcane. Between the two of them they managed to strap on the heavy double saddle without waking any of the drivers. They climbed on its back and Jodril urged the reluctant beast to its feet. Munching the sweetcane it plodded forward, its head weaving to and fro in a puzzled way. Silently they left the oasis and traveled north, skirting the sleeping village. At the foot of the Great Dune they dismounted and left the kneeling kroklyn hobbled, so that it could not return to the others without them.

The stars blazed whitely and in their light Antia could just see the curve of the dune against the sky, like a frozen wave poised above their heads. They began to climb. Below them the kroklyn snuffled suddenly, a startlingly loud sound in the silence.

"What's bothering it?" Jodril muttered. "Hope it settles down or it'll wake someone in the village and they'll come up to see what's wrong."

"What now?" whispered Antia, when at last they reached the crest of the dune and could look down into the pool of blackness that was the valley beyond.

"We wait." Jodril placed the bundle he had brought with him carefully beside him on the sand, slipped off his sandals, and sat cross-legged on the ground, his face almost hidden by the hood of his robe.

"Wait for what?"

"For the dawn. Be still."

Antia sat beside him, trying to find a comfortable posture on the hard windblown sand. It was cold, dark, and silent, and the brilliant stars were no comfort at all. Be still, he had said. In spite of herself, she shivered. Jodril never stirred.

After what seemed like a hundred years, she noticed that the sky in the east was not as black as it had been, that she could count fewer stars in that quarter. Then, slowly, the whole vault of the sky turned a deep blue. A cold wind stirred the sand atop the ridge. She shivered again.

With tropic suddenness the sun leaped like a giant red ball above the horizon. The desert, which had vanished in the blackness of the night, leaped back into existence in a harsh jangle of light and shadow. Directly below where they sat the shadow of the handar, that strange wind-carved pillar, stretched across the valley floor.

"Now!" Jodril picked up his bundle and plunged barefooted down the farther slope with Antia at his heels. The sand was cold and rough under her feet. She could feel her toes shrinking back from it.

At the base of the handar Jodril unwrapped his mysterious bundle. Why, it was nothing more than a simple woven basket piled with fruit, not even exotic fruit, but the simple dates and pomegranates that the peasants ate. He placed it on the ground, bowed so deeply that his head touched the sand, and then walked backward to the foot of the dune.

"What now?" Antia whispered.

"Either Sandwriter will come or she will not."

"And how will we know?"

"We will wait."

Oh, no, thought Antia. More waiting! She tried to imitate Jodril's position, cross-legged, straight-backed, facing north toward the rugged red of the cliff behind the handar. After a few minutes her thigh muscles screamed in agony and she had to shift to another position.

"S-ssh," whispered Jodril. "Be still."

His eyes were on the ground, his hands lightly folded in his lap. His face looked strangely empty, as if *he* had gone somewhere else, thought Antia. Her nose began to itch. She tried to concentrate on the cliff opposite. Its red rock was smoothed by sand and wind, but was curiously pockmarked with shadows. After a time she realized that these shadows must be fissures or even the openings to caves. It's riddled with them, she thought idly. Like a piece of cheese.

The sun's light was now reflected from the dune to the cliff face opposite. Her eyes began to water and she shut them. When she opened them again she found that she was now looking at something immediately in front of her. She focused. The rough texture of homespun. Beneath the ragged hem two bare feet, hard with walking, knotted with age. She looked up slowly, her heart beating fast. The face was shadowed, hidden by the hood of the robe.

"So you have returned. This time you shall see and understand. Come." The woman turned away as Antia and Jodril scrambled to their feet.

"But, Lady . . ." Jodril stammered. She turned. Antia saw her eyes flash. "We have come to tell you . . . to ask for help . . . Roshan has been betrayed."

"By me," Antia interrupted. "I'm sorry. I didn't mean . . ."

Her words faded into silence as the woman turned again and walked across the valley toward the base of the cliff. At the foot of the handar, Jodril's gift lay untouched. With a small movement Sandwriter gestured and he bent to pick up the basket.

At the base of the cliff she stopped and made another gesture. "Here is the heart of Roshan. Tell me the way in."

"I cannot, Lady," Jodril answered. "I have not seen it, only heard of it."

"And you?" She turned to Antia.

"I don't know. Maybe . . . yes, that big opening directly behind the pillar. Is the pillar a sign?"

"There are signs, but the skill is in interpreting them. If you were to go into *that* passage you would find yourself in a maze, winding tighter and tighter in toward its center, which is nothing. If you were fortunate you might find your way out again."

"Well, then, that one over there." Why was the old woman playing games with them?

"Beyond that opening is a straight passage. A hundred paces along is a pit. Beyond the pit is a blank wall."

"Then I don't know. How can I possibly guess? There are hundreds of openings and cracks. It could be any of them."

"You told me that you had betrayed the secret of Roshan. Yet how could you do so when you do not even know its beginning? Be at peace, child. It was not your fault and no harm is done."

But there *is*. You don't know Eskoril, thought Antia. "There is," she said aloud, but the old woman had turned away and was striding surefootedly over the rocks and rubble that strewed the cliff base.

"Walk as I walk," she told them, and then they noticed that she stepped from rock to rock, her feet never touching the sand, so that there was no trail of betraying footprints.

Antia concentrated on stepping from stone to stone, and when she looked up again she cried out in surprise. Sandwriter had vanished.

"Truth is not always obvious." A voice spoke hollowly from a cleft so narrow that it did not seem possible that it could be the entrance to a cave. "Nor is it always easy. It takes hard work and sometimes danger to discern the truth. Come. Trust me. Step sideways with your shoulder to the crack. Keep your chin tucked down against your other shoulder."

Antia felt stone tighten around her. It was very dark. There was a smell of ancient dust. Suppose I get stuck. Suppose there should be a rockfall. After all, something brought down those stones out there in the valley. Suppose . . .

A more terrifying thought struck her. Perhaps this was a trap. Perhaps she was to be shut up in the cliff forever as a punishment for being a spy, a traitor to Roshan. Jodril would be in on it and the Chief. In spite of the chill, sweat ran down her face. She tried to raise a hand to wipe it away, but her hand was jammed against her side.

In panic, she wriggled desperately sideways. Suddenly the pressure on ribs and shoulders lessened. Another few steps and she was able to stand upright and move her hands freely to feel the texture of cold rough rock about her. Blackness. And silence.

"Is anyone there?" she whispered in terror. "Anyone?"

"There is nothing."

Where did the voice come from? Was it from in front, or over there to the side? She strained her eyes into the darkness.

The voice began again. "Nothingness is the first lesson of the caves. The first step in wisdom is being aware that one knows nothing. We must leave behind all prejudice, all mis-understanding, all misinformation, all lies. In the first dark-ness of the rock of Roshan we are all like unborn children. Now we must be born into the light."

There was the scratching sound of flint and steel. A spark, enormous in the darkness, lasted for too brief a time for her to discern anything. Then a torch flared and the reality of the three-dimensional world was back.

A rough wooden bale was thrust into Antia's hand. Its hollow top was filled with some sticky black substance that burned with a dusky orange flame and a lot of black smoke. She held it high and saw that she was standing against the wall of a cave, wide and long, whose vaulted ceiling was too high to reflect the glimmer of her torch. Ahead was more darkness, suddenly illuminated by the torch Sandwriter held high. She beckoned to them and turned.

At first Antia tried to keep in her mind some mental picture of where they were going, but there were so many forks in the path, so many twists and turns, that she gave up and concentrated only on following the light ahead. All the time they were descending. At one point there was a pit, rounded out by a lava flow of long ago, with a rope ladder affixed to its wall.

I cannot possibly go down there, Antia told herself. But it was that or remain alone in the darkness that lurked just beyond the torches' reach. She climbed grimly down, clinging to the twisting ladder with her feet and one hand, while her other hand desperately clutched the torch.

The air, which had at first struck chill, was now getting uncomfortably warm. They splashed across a shallow stream and Antia cried out in surprise because the water was hot. They passed cracks in the rock from which came puffs of hot air, heavy and sulfurous, that stirred her stomach uneasily.

Then they came upon a narrow bridge of rock, a natural neck that was all that remained of the roof of some cave far below. When she held out her torch it showed only blackness on either side. Whether the drop was two meters or two hundred she had no way of telling. Suppose I slip, she thought. But she followed Sandwriter, fear drying her mouth. She did not slip, and beyond the bridge the going was smooth and the path brushed clean.

Antia was numb with fear and exhaustion by the time Sandwriter halted, and she knew they must have reached the place that was the heart of Roshan. They were in a wide, high cave, with fresh air coming in from somewhere far above. There was the sweet smell of fresh water and when she held up her torch she could see it, dark and still. Behind it a curtain of stone rippled as if it too were made of water. She turned and light winked in a thousand jewel colors from pillars and bosses.

She let out her breath in a long happy sigh. "I wasn't mad. I didn't dream it. It *is* all real."

Jodril turned on her. "You told Eskoril of *this*?"

Her hand went to her mouth. "I did. Yes, I did. I told him everything I remembered about this place."

"You must tell me about this Eskoril." Sandwriter spoke quietly.

"He is a Kamalant spy," Jodril interrupted.

Sandwriter held up her hand in silent rebuke and turned to Antia. "Who is this man?"

Again Antia had to explain. ". . . and I still cannot believe that he is evil. He wants something for himself, something to do with the cave and the pools. Only I do not know what it can be."

"For himself? Not for Kamalant?"

"I think so. He . . . he did not like to be only a tutor. He wanted more." She felt her face burn in the shadows.

"Did you not think that you were destroying truth when you deceived us, as our guest and friend?"

"Yes. No. A little maybe. But he is my friend, too. I wanted to help him."

"There was no truth in you, was there?"

"No. I . . . "

"Though you had been bathed in the water of Roshan?"

"I didn't know it was something special. I thought it was just water."

"And so it is. Just water. The most precious thing on Roshan. The wellspring. The heartland of the world."

"I'm sorry. You're just not making any sense." Antia blinked and sniffed. "I am sorry I told Eskoril. Afterward I tried to tell him that I had been making it up, but he didn't believe me."

109

In the silence that followed, Antia trembled. Now comes the sentence, she thought. And the punishment. If they leave me here I won't be able to bear it. I shall go mad.

"Take her torch, Jodril, son of Hamrab," said Sandwriter in a most ordinary voice. "Put it and yours in those sconces over there. Come and sit down. We will share this basket of delicious fruit you have brought. Come now!"

Unbelievingly, Antia sat. She ate the fruit, tasting nothing. She drank a cup of sweet, cold spring water. When the silent meal was finished, Sandwriter gazed for a long time into the pool. Now and then the water trembled as the slow spring seeped upward.

"Now listen to me," she said at last. "For I will tell you a story."

In the beginning, the world of Rokam was a great ball of hot rock, so hot that nothing could live upon it. Then the First One sent the rain gods to Rokam. It rained, rain such as you could not even imagine. Thunder rolled from side to side and lightning tore apart the sky. Out of this chasm came more rain. It rained for hundreds of years.

As the hot rock began to steam, the storms became even more violent. Slowly the rocks cooled and crumpled. Water began to collect in the low parts and this became the Great Sea. As it went on raining, the water began to rise until, by the time it finally stopped and the sun at last showed itself, half of Rokam was beneath the sea. All that remained were the twin continents of Kamalant and Komilant, the island of Roshan and the Far Islands in the midst of the Great Sea.

Once the rocks had cooled and the sun had come out, green things began to grow. Grasses and trees and flowering bushes flourished in all the lands of Rokam, and it was most beautiful. And the first men appeared on Rokam. They were brothers, and their names were Antan, Baleth, and Calman.

The eldest brother, who was the most clever, claimed the great continent of Kamalant, while the second brother, who was almost as clever, claimed Komilant. This left the island of

Roshan for the youngest, Calman, who was a poet and a dreamer and not in the least bit clever like his brothers.

Together Antan and Baleth devised a magic which forced all the rain clouds that rolled around Rokam from west to east to shed their rain on the twin continents. Then the trees on Kamalant and Komilant grew taller and the grass was as high as a man, so that the people on the twin continents flourished.

But by the time they reached Roshan the clouds were wrung dry, and little or no rain fell. The trees and shrubs withered and dwindled away. Every year there was less vegetation. Even the grass failed and the earth dried up and blew away and left only sand. From the heart of Roshan this desert slowly ate its way, like a disease, across the island. The people began to crowd along the coast, because that was the only place left where they could live. And even on the coast they began to get hungry.

When Calman saw what had happened, he asked his brothers to release some of the rain so that Roshan might flourish once again. But they laughed at him. Then Calman became angry. "Very well," he told his people. "I will go out into the desert and I will seek out the rain gods and ask them to have pity on us."

The people of Roshan said, "Don't go. You will die out there. There are no figs or dates to eat and no water to drink. There is nothing."

Calman was young and frail, but he was very angry and this made him brave. "Nevertheless, I will go," he said. "If I die, my death will be on the heads of the gods."

He left the people of Roshan and, with nothing but a hooded robe to shelter his body from the sun and sandals to protect his feet from the burning sand, he set out to find the heart of Roshan so that he might speak to the gods.

He walked for days. His head throbbed and his eyes burned with the heat. His tongue and lips swelled up so that he could

112

hardly have spoken if there had been anyone to speak to. But there was nobody. After many days, he noticed that the sun was directly over his head, so that his body made not the smallest shadow at noon. Then he knew that he had reached the heart of Roshan.

He squatted on the sand and waited for the rain gods to notice him. The sun set and the stars shone brilliantly in the cloudless sky, as many as there were grains of sand in the desert below. He waited.

The sun rose and climbed up the dome of the sky until it was directly overhead. He saw again that his body made not the smallest shadow in any direction, and he knew that he had indeed stopped at the right place. But still the rain gods did not come.

The sun set and the stars came out, though Calman was too weak to lift up his head and see their brilliance. He sat on the burning sand with his head bowed and thought sadly: My people were right. I was a fool to come. I shall die in the heart of Roshan and all for nothing. The rain gods are too busy listening to my clever brothers to pay any attention to me.

When dawn came again he tried to cry out one last word of reproach to the rain gods, but his throat was as dry as the sand. They never even heard my voice, he thought bitterly.

At that moment a single drop of rain fell on the back of his hand. He bent his head to it and felt its sweetness against his dry lips. Another drop fell and he touched it with his tongue.

"Listen to me, rain gods," he whispered. "Let me die, but save my people. Save Roshan." His head sank onto his chest and he prepared for death.

"Look up." A shimmering voice came to him from left and right and above and in front. He looked up and blinked, thinking he must be already dead.

Standing before him, but not standing, for their feet did not touch the sand, were three beings. He could not tell if they

113

were male or female. They were dressed alike in robes that fell as straight as silk and were of a color that was not quite green and not quite blue and not quite gray. Their eyes were blue. Or were they perhaps green or gray? It was difficult to tell.

They spoke together in low melodious voices. "Calman, son of Rokam, what do you want?"

"Justice," he whispered hoarsely. "Enough water to save my people from death. No more. But you have given so much to Kamalant and Komilant that there is nothing left for Roshan."

"Your brothers Antan and Baleth did not ask us for water. They tricked it from us by magic. They are very clever and very powerful. One day they will learn the secrets of the earth gods, too, and they will take from them everything they want. The forests will get in the way of the earth and they will cut them down. Still we will have to give them the rain they tricked from us. But then it will wash away the soil down the rivers to the ocean, until all the good earth is gone. Because they took without asking. Because they were born clever, but without wisdom."

Calman bowed his head wordlessly. His heart was full of sadness for his own people and for his foolish clever brothers.

"We have little left to give you," the voices went on. "But what we have is yours."

He looked up in hope and saw the three standing together with their right hands raised to the sky and their left hands pointing down to the ground. Then out of the four corners of the world came the wind and on the wind came clouds. And it began to rain.

Calman tore off his robe and threw it aside. He stood with his arms outstretched and felt the rain on his body. He threw back his head and opened his dry mouth to it, rejoicing.

At length the three dropped their arms. At once the clouds rolled back to the four corners of the world. The sky was blue and the sun shone directly overhead so that Calman's body made not the smallest shadow. He looked around. From horizon to horizon the dry sand stretched out. "Where is the water you promised?" he stammered.

"Underneath," the voices shimmered. "Underneath, where it will be safe. Use it wisely. Learn to live with what Roshan can give you and our gift will last forever."

"How will I find this place again? It is like all the other places around."

"Leave your robe to mark the spot. It will show the heart of Roshan to those whom you choose to tell."

The figures became thin, began to waver like a mirage, to drift apart like mist.

"Wait! I don't understand. You say we must have wisdom. But I need knowledge too, knowledge like that of my brothers. For the sake of my people I ask it."

The three rain gods sighed and it was like the wind that brings the storm. "Since you have asked we will give it to you. It is also hidden beneath the ground. But beware, Calman. Without wisdom this knowledge may well destroy Roshan."

"I don't understand . . . " he shouted, because by now the figures seemed to be a great way off. "How can I tell the difference between wisdom and knowledge?"

"Knowledge helps men." The voices were very faint. "Wisdom helps humankind."

A sudden wind whipped a pillar of sand into the air. Calman strained his eyes but he could no longer see the rain gods. He was alone. He looked around wonderingly. Where he had dropped his brown robe a great rock reared up out of the ground. And, instead of falling, the pillar of sand stood frozen in front of it, in the shape of a handar.

He knew that by these signs he would always be able to find the heart of Roshan and its secret wealth. He walked back

115

across the desert to his people, turning over in his mind all the things he had been told.

In the silence of the cave a drop of water fell from the ceiling into the pool below. Antia watched the slow circles spread outward.

"Is this all that remains of the water that the rain gods gave to Calman?" Jodril asked.

Sandwriter looked up at him. "You know how the desert blooms after rain. When you see the buds swell and open in one place you know, without having to go and see for yourself, that wherever the rain has fallen the flowers will bloom. This pool, at the heart of Roshan, is a sign. But there are many others. I alone hold the secret, and I will tell it only to the one who is to come after me."

"You mean there's more water?" Antia forgot her awe of Sandwriter in her eagerness to share her knowledge. "Why, that means you could build cities out here in the desert. You can sink wells. With wind-powered pumps you could make the desert bloom all year round, not just after the rain . . ."

She stopped, for now Sandwriter stood up, her hood thrown back to show the heavy white hair above the strong brow. Her eyes flashed and Antia drew back. But Sandwriter's voice was gentle. "You speak with the voice of Kamalant, child. Tell me, what would the people in these great new cities do once the water was used up?"

"Dig deeper, I suppose. There're probably masses of water underground, enough to last forever. The rest . . . well, that was just a story, wasn't it?"

"A story? There is no wisdom in your words, child. Roshan survives because the Chiefs have always heeded the words of Calman when he came back from talking with the rain gods. The cities on the coast are very small. At each oasis no more people may live than can do so with what Roshan gives them freely. There is a beetle that we call the calman beetle. It lives on the fringes of the desert. Every dawn it holds up its hairy legs to catch the dew. On that dew it lives throughout the heat of the day. We Roshanites are like the calman beetle. We catch the small dew. We survive."

"You'll never get rich and powerful that way."

"Like Kamalant?" Jodril scorned.

"Yes, like Kamalant." She turned on him. "Don't tell me you wouldn't like to be rich and powerful when you are Chief, Jodril. To rule over many people, to have all the luxuries we have."

"I've never thought about it."

"That's not wisdom. That's just laziness."

Sandwriter laughed. "She is right, Jodril. You must learn to think for yourself. This moment should have followed your eighteenth birthday, but these are strange times. Come, both of you. I will reveal to you the power of Roshan. Then you may judge for yourself."

She took a torch from one of the sconces set in the cave wall and walked swiftly away into the darkness. "Come." She beckoned them, bent and slid into a cleft in the far wall. Jodril and Antia followed close behind.

Down a long twisting passage they went, and then another. Again it became hot. Finally they reached another cave, also with a pool at its center, like a dark shining eye.

"You have seen the wisdom of Roshan," Sandwriter said softly, holding her torch high above the black water. "Here is its cleverness." As she finished speaking, she dipped her torch toward the water.

"No, don't!" Jodril and Antia cried out together. Sandwriter held the only torch. If it was extinguished they would be in darkness and how could they ever find their way back?

Then they cried out again, in fear and surprise, for the torch did not go out. Instead flames left the torch and ran out across the surface of the water, blue and orange flame, vanishing and reappearing as they watched.

Even while superstitious fear made the hair on Antia's arms prickle, a small voice inside her head said coolly: This is nothing so strange. You have seen something like this before.

Jodril fell to his knees and covered his head with his robe. "The earth gods have come!"

"These are no gods." Sandwriter's voice was scornful. "Get up, boy. Kneel before the living water if you wish, but do not kneel here. This is the other gift that the rain gods gave unwillingly to Calman, because he begged them for it. This is power. One day it may well destroy Roshan."

Power. Antia remembered where she had seen a sight like this before, in the Luminar Marshes on the edge of the rain forests of Komilant. Ghost lights flickering in the night, and a strange smell, not unlike the smell in this cave.

Curious, she knelt and touched the surface of the water. She found that the blackness was not a sign of the depth of the liquid but was a part of the liquid itself, as if it were paint or mud. She smelled her fingertips, wrinkled her nose, and rubbed her fingers clean against the front of her robe. It was thick and hard to get off.

"I know this stuff, though I forget what they call it. There is some of it in Komilant and the wise men are looking for ways to make it as clean as water. Then they say it will be the most powerful stuff on Rokam. That it will run everything. We will no longer need animals or sunpower or the wind or anything."

"Will the sun and the wind go away when you no longer need them? What you are suggesting is foolishness, Antia. We already have what we need."

"Then sell this stuff to Kamalant. Why, I'm sure we'd give you anything you want for it . . . oh!"

"What is it?"

118

"I've just realized . . . for a moment I had forgotten . . . Eskoril. *This* must be what he wants. *This* is what he tricked me into spying for!"

"And you've told him all he needs to know." Jodril's face was grim.

"Oh, Jodril, maybe he'll believe what I said, that I'd made it up, that it was just dreams. . . ."

Her voice faded as Jodril shook his head. "He must have a clear idea of what lies beneath Roshan or he would never have gone to the risk of involving you. If Kamalant wants what is ours, I fear for Roshan."

Antia tried to laugh. "Why, Uncle Rangor wouldn't hurt a fly."

"Perhaps. But what about his younger brother, Kayteth? And, forgive me, Antia, but what about your aunt, the Queen?"

She nodded unhappily. Aunt Sankath certainly craved power. As for Uncle Kayteth . . . She remembered her last visit to Komilant. Her uncle, with blotched face, small red eyes, and unsteady hands, was not clever. But he was vain and envious. He could be used.

By whom? That was the question.

The answer came into her mind as clearly as if someone had spoken it out loud. Eskoril. Eskoril and the Queen. And she, Antia, had been their dupe all these months. She dropped her head into her hands.

"You have discovered the truth?" Sandwriter spoke out of the shadows cast by the flickering torch.

"Yes. Oh, what am I to do? There must be something, even now . . ."

"Let action remain in the hands of the powerful. Wait and see. Grow strong inside. And remember that you can always tell the difference between knowledge and wisdom. Wisdom never forgets love."

119

She led them up the dark ways to the big cave, across it and through the winding passages until at last they came out unexpectedly into the valley between the cliff and the Great Dune.

Jodril knelt before the bent figure of Sandwriter. After a moment's hesitation so did Antia. She felt a hand lightly touch her head. When she looked up again they were alone.

Jodril was already scrambling up the side of the dune.

"Wait for me."

He waited, but said nothing. His face was stormy.

"Jodril, don't look at me like that."

"I can't help it. I know he tricked you, that none of this is really your fault. But to see for the first time in my life the glory of Roshan's secret and to know that it is in the hands of a man like that . . . it is just too much to bear."

"I'm sorry. I'm really sorry. Jodril, don't be unkind to me. Remember what Sandwriter said: 'Wisdom never forgets love!' And she trusted me. She showed me the black pool. She didn't have to."

He looked at her, his eyes hard. "The ways of oracles are strange." He shrugged. "Come on. We must get back to the oasis."

He climbed the dune ahead of her, waited silently by the kroklyn until she had scrambled into the saddle, and then kicked it to its feet. It had been dawn when they first met Sandwriter. It was now nearly noon. The air shimmered with the heat and the sun lay heavily across the land.

When they finally got to the oasis, Antia collapsed under a tree. After Jodril had looked after the kroklyn, he brought her a cup of water and a handful of dates, but he didn't stay to eat his own lunch with her. He went off to where the drivers were resting. She could hear their voices, low and lazy in the heat of the afternoon. Now and then the rattle of dice and a shout of laughter.

120

The heat made her head ache and the shimmer of hot air beyond the oasis made her feel as if she had a fever, as if it had all been a strange dream. She turned over and over in her mind the events of that morning. The clear pool. The black pool. Wisdom. Knowledge.

Was power wrong? Or only if you used it wrongfully? To Jodril it was all as simple as the desert itself. Why couldn't he see things from her point of view for once? Oh, I wish he'd talk to me. I wish we could be friends again.

Affairs of state. It seemed so exciting, the way Eskoril explained it to me. He made me feel so important. Oh, Eskoril, how could you? But I was wrong too. I didn't have to agree. Only I trusted him . . .

Her thoughts wove around and around in a tight unhappy circle. She rolled over onto her front with a sniff and buried her head on her arms.

Someone was shaking her shoulder. "Miss, miss, wake up." A strange voice, heavily accented.

She rolled over and blinked up at the shadowy figure, his back to the sun. It was one of the drivers. "What is it?"

He put a finger to his lips. She stared. His dark face was shadowed as well by the deep folds of his hood. She sat up and looked around. It was still very hot, perhaps a couple of hours after noon. In the shaded oasis no one stirred. Even the kroklyns slept.

"The young Chief wishes you to come."

"Jodril?" She got to her feet, blinking the sleep out of her eyes. Her head still throbbed and she couldn't think clearly. "Where?"

"He has gone back to the valley. He wants me to take you to him. He says it is urgent." The man's voice was low and his accent made it difficult for her to follow.

"But why didn't he wait for me? It doesn't make sense."

121

"It is urgent," he repeated. Antia shrugged irritably. He probably doesn't understand me anyway, she thought, as she followed the robed figure to the northern edge of the oasis, where a kroklyn knelt, ready to be mounted.

As they rode past the sleeping village, up toward the crested dune, her questions fell away and she began to be happy. Whatever it is, Jodril wants me to be part of it. So he has forgiven me, after all.

The driver forced the kroklyn's head east and led them around the trailing edge of the dune. Here, at the foot of the valley, they dismounted.

Antia looked around. The red cliffs shimmered in the heat. Overhead a bird of prey circled on large leathery-looking wings. Sweat ran down her face and neck. She wiped them and looked around. "Where is Jodril? The young Chief? You said . . ."

"He wishes you to meet him in the cave where you were this morning." His accent made it difficult for her to understand. She made him tell her again.

"How strange. Why didn't he wait for me out here?"

The man shrugged and spread out his hands.

"Oh, all right. Go ahead."

"After you, young miss."

"But . . ." He had led the way to the kroklyn. He had led the way into the valley. Now he wished *her* to lead? A small icy suspicion began to grow inside her. She didn't look at his face but down at the ground. She waited obstinately for him to take the lead. She could feel his eyes on her and she was suddenly very afraid. They were a long way from anyone else. She stared at the sand, finding herself thinking idly: There is something odd about this man's footprints. What is it?

"Miss, the young Chief is waiting."

"You go first. Show me the way."

"You must know that I do not know it." There was anger,

barely concealed, in the voice. Antia looked up. Jodril was nowhere in sight. The long valley looked very empty. Above their heads the birds still circled.

She shivered and clenched her hands so that the nails dug into her palms. She tried to keep her voice cool and steady. "Very well. You may leave me now. I will go on and meet the young Chief. Take the kroklyn back to the oasis."

He shook his head as if he did not understand and waited impassively for her to go ahead. She walked past him, just a few steps along the valley. When she turned back he hadn't moved.

"Leave!" She stamped her foot. "I will not go until you have taken the kroklyn back around the dune."

"The young Chief told me to stay with you, miss."

Jodril would never have said that. Jodril, who of all people, knew the importance of keeping secret the way into the caves. "Who are you?" she asked sharply.

"A kroklyn driver, miss. You know that. My name is Shad." His voice somehow mocked her.

Something is wrong. I mustn't stay here. I must go back to the oasis. But will he let me? Oh, where is Jodril? She looked along the valley again and then back the way they had come. At her footprints small in the sand. And the driver's beside hers. Heavier on the left side than the right. The footprints of a man who limped.

In spite of the blazing heat Antia felt icy cold. She understood fully now the terrible danger she was in.

# 9

Antia forced her eyes away from the telltale footprints. She took a deep steadying breath and walked quickly back, past the driver, toward the eastern end of the valley. As she passed him his robe brushed against her arm. She shivered, wanting to run, forcing herself not to. She had only taken ten steps past him before he had caught up with her.

"Where are you going?" He held her wrist in a strong brown hand, a hand tanned from years of desert living. I must be wrong, she thought. Other men limp. I was crazy to think . . . She could smell the kroklyn smell on him. Under it was another unexpected, somehow familiar scent. What was it?

"Where are you going?" he repeated.

"Let go of me. You forget yourself."

"Miss, you must go into the cave to meet the young Chief."

"I don't believe Jodril sent you. I'm going back to the oasis."

She tried to pull her arm free, but his grip tightened. Then, so suddenly that she gasped, he pulled her toward him and twisted her arm behind her back. Her shoulder hurt agonizingly and sweat ran down her face. Don't let me faint, she prayed. Don't let me show any weakness.

"You will take me to the cave. You will show me the way."

"Jodril's not there at all, is he? There never was a message."

He smiled. She caught the flash of white teeth from the shadow of his hood. "I must see the cave. Come."

"No. I will not. Let me go."

He twisted her hand up against her shoulder blade and this time she couldn't stop herself from screaming. She fell to her knees and mercifully he relaxed his grip. *Perhaps I could pretend to have fainted. Perhaps he will be afraid then and go away.* She slumped over to the hot sand and kept her eyes shut.

A foot touched her ribs. "Get up, Princess. I know you are pretending. Up, I say." The foot pushed against her side.

*I cannot let him* kick *me,* she thought, and got slowly to her feet. Her shoulder ached and she wondered if it were dislocated.

"You are going to show me. If you do not, then I shall hurt you again. Is that clear?"

"Yes."

"Go on, then."

Slowly she walked along the valley, close to the fallen rocks that strewed the foot of the cliff. Her mind raced. When she came to the wind-carved pillar of sandstone she paused, just for an instant, and then walked briskly westward along the valley. Would he notice?

"Stop!"

Her heart thumped. He had fallen for it. She turned slowly. He stood in the full light of the afternoon sun and she stared at his face, shadowed by the hood. Did she recognize him? Was it he?

"Come back."

She walked back, her eyes downcast, hoping that her face gave nothing away. She suddenly remembered Eskoril teaching her to play castles, long ago in the palace garden, when he was a tutor and she a child, ignorant of everything except the fact that she loved him. He used to laugh when he won, telling her that her face was like a mirror. She hoped that she had learned to conceal her feelings a little better since then.

"Do you take me for an idiot?" In his anger the thick accent of the kroklyn driver was slipping and she could hear the clipped voice beneath. "We will go this way."

"It's not the entrance." She stared at him, trying to show fear and a hidden cunning.

"I will see for myself. Come. You will go first."

She let her shoulders sag, as if in despair, and slipped obediently into the cleft behind the handar. It was very narrow, but opened almost immediately into a large space. Blinded by the darkness after the brilliant sun, she stood still.

"What are you waiting for? Go on."

"I can't see a thing. I hope you brought a light with you." She let her voice sound sulky, as if acknowledging that he had already won. Perhaps, just perhaps, he might get careless and make a mistake. What had Sandwriter said? "A maze, winding tighter and tighter in toward its center, which is nothing. If you were fortunate you might find your way out again."

If they were to lose their way they would both die. The thought made her so afraid she wasn't sure she could bear it; but at least the secret of Roshan would be safe. She tried to think of Calman. He had been willing to die . . .

A rod of light pierced the blackness behind her. A Kamalant torch, an artifact hardly likely to find its way into the hands of a humble kroklyn driver. So it *was* he, in spite of the robes and the brown arms. She no longer felt angry but very sad.

"Lead the way. You can see perfectly now. Come. I have no time to waste."

"I don't know the way. I told you – this isn't the right passage."

"Shall I hurt you again?"

"No. Please, no!" She crossed the entrance cave and entered

the passage in the far wall. Turning left and right, it seemed to lead into the heart of the mountain. She took the turns at random, not wanting to remember the way back. At length the passage ended in a blank wall.

He swore. "You are being deliberately stupid. Perhaps I should twist your other arm."

"I told you I don't know the way. Why won't you believe me? And I don't know the way out either." She turned to face him boldly. He played the beam of light over her face. She put up her hand to shield her eyes.

The light moved away. She heard him laugh shortly. "Come. We will go back and try again."

When they came to a fork in the passage she turned to the left. He pulled her back. "Where do you think you're going?"

"Isn't this the way we came?"

"No. It was the one to the right."

The same thing happened at the next division in the passage. This time the light showed her the chalk mark he had made on the wall. He had won. Wordlessly she followed him as he threaded his way unerringly through the maze and out into the shimmering heat of the valley.

"Shall we try again?"

At the next cleft in the rock he pushed her ahead of him. "No, don't. I know this isn't right. It's a . . . " She bit back the words. How many paces had Sandwriter said? His hand was on the small of her back. She ducked and drew back, trembling, against the side wall. He took a pace past her and his torch showed only blackness instead of the rocky floor ahead. He played the light downward and then laughed.

"It's lucky I still need you, Princess." He caught her arm, pushed her toward the edge, and then, as she screamed, pulled her back toward him. He laughed again.

Back in sunlight Antia felt as if she had wakened from a nightmare. It was all so ordinary. The sun shone. The rocks reflected its light. The blue sky, like a lid, seemed to trap the heat. The bird still flew in slow wide circles. Oh, *where* was Jodril? If only he would come. Together they could overcome this man.

"On!" His now hateful voice goaded her. She walked slowly westward. The next opening was the real one. It was narrower even than the others, so insignificant that she had not seen it even when Sandwriter vanished into it. Perhaps . . . She plodded on by, her heart beating so hard that she was sure he must hear it.

"Stop!"

"What is it?"

"Did you forget this one?"

"It's so small. Only a crack. It can't be the one."

"Three times lucky perhaps." He pushed her ahead of him into the fissure. She smelled that strange odor again, kroklyns and . . . brakawood perfume. That was it. Faint, but quite unmistakable. Again, that sad sense of regret. That it should be him.

"It's too small. You can see I can't possibly get through there. You'll stick and then we'll both be trapped." She let her voice get shrill, as if in real distress. It wasn't difficult. She wanted to weep.

He played the light over the walls, crouched, and let it run along the ground ahead of them. "There are footprints. Someone has been this way. If they can, then so can we." His hand propelled her into the narrow fissure.

She wriggled through, hoping that he might indeed get stuck. But he was slim, unlike most Kamalantans, and he got through with no more difficulty than she had.

As they stood in the cave within she could hear his breath, harsh and loud. He laughed, but his laughter did not ring true. He tried to illuminate the vastness of the entrance cave with his torch. The ellipse of light touched ceiling, walls, floor, the

128

darkness of an opening. But all only suggested, touched on. Nothing whole or at one time.

He cleared his throat and she could feel his unease. "Lead the way, Antia, my dear." Now he had her in the cave he wasn't even pretending to be the driver anymore. All right. She wouldn't pretend either.

"You know what a dreadful memory I have, Eskoril. I honestly don't know if I can find the way."

His laughter was forced. "How long have you known?"

"Almost from the beginning. You're not a very good actor." He was off balance. She must try to keep him that way. She must find his weakness and use it against him. Then maybe . . .

"Why did you say nothing sooner?"

"It was amusing to see my tutor trying to play the part of a flea-bitten kroklyn driver. It quite suited you, Eskoril."

He slapped her face. The outrage was harder to bear than the pain, but she pretended it was nothing. Every tiny prick that sent him a little more off balance was in her favor.

He pushed back his hood. She saw sweat glisten on his forehead. Yet it was chilly in here. She could feel the prickles of gooseflesh on her arms. What was he afraid of? Her? Or something else?

A plan, vague as morning mist, drifted into her mind. "So now you no longer have to pretend." She tried to keep her voice light, amused. "Tell me what you have been doing since I left Kamalant all those weeks ago? You've been in Roshan all along, I suppose."

He was silent. Then he laughed briefly. "I came on the ship following yours. It was quicker and I was here by the time you landed."

"Why did you need me, since you were doing your own spying?"

"I could hardly come to Roshan uninvited as the royal tutor.

129

Questions would have been asked. And as a nobody, doors would be shut in my face that opened automatically for you. But I had my own sources of information. Just as well. It was very naughty of you to lie to me about the caves, my dear Antia."

"You may address me as Princess, Eskoril." Her voice was cold, but she kept her temper. He doesn't want to explore the caves, though he knows he must. That's why he's content to stand here talking to me. He's afraid of the dark. Afraid of caves!

"So now you know the secret of Roshan, what are you going to do with it?" she asked. "How long have you suspected something like this? It must have been for years. All the time you were my tutor you were planning to use me."

He laughed. "You're right. More than seven years ago I met a young man from Komilant who had traveled to Roshan. He talked a great deal about his travels, fascinating stuff. So I took him to an inn and gave him a great deal of wine. And he told me what he had discovered of the secret at the heart of Roshan."

"A story."

"A story that could make my fortune, bring me the power I needed."

"But it belongs to Roshan."

"For the moment it does. It is not important."

He was so casual. She bit the inside of her lip and then went on. "So what happened next? Did the young man bring you to Roshan to show you. . . ?" She stopped as he shook his head. His teeth gleamed as he smiled.

"He had altogether too many uncomfortable ideals. He wasn't a practical man at all. So I had to cut the tie. Poor boy."

The skin of her face tightened with fear. "You mean you . . . ? Yes, I see. You would, wouldn't you?"

"I think you do see, Princess. Kamalant will be all-

130

powerful. Nothing will be able to stand in our way. We will have it all."

"But we have so much already!"

"My dear, you sound almost like a Roshanite. The simple life, with just enough for each person and no more than you need. What a bore! I would rather have everything."

Antia swallowed, suddenly feeling sick. This was the man she had been in love with, for whom she had risked her honor and the security of Roshan? For this self-serving creature. . . .

But was I any better? She licked dry lips. "In the rose garden – when you asked me to help you – I thought it was something that would get you a better job, make you more important."

He laughed. "And so it will. The Queen is impatient with the way her husband rules Kamalant."

"The Queen! So you are a traitor to King Rangor, to Kamalant, as well as everything else!"

"Words, words. Once I was a nobody, Princess. Then I whispered the story of Roshan's power into the Queen's ears. She listened. I was appointed your tutor. You became very fond of me. So did she."

His caressing tone brought color flooding to Antia's cheeks. That she should have been so blind, so stupid, as to be in love with this . . . this snake! She clenched her hands, thankful that the darkness hid her face. His voice continued, mockingly.

"The King, your uncle, is in poor health. He eats and drinks too much and has the gout. Once out of the way the Queen will marry his brother, Prince Kayteth. They will rule the twin continents together."

"What's in it for you?"

"How crudely you put it. Life on Roshan has vulgarized you, my dear. As I said, the Queen is exceedingly fond of me. I shall be the power next to the throne."

Oh, how I hate you, she thought. She managed a small

131

scornful laugh. "How strange, Eskoril. I had thought you would have chosen to *be* the throne."

There was silence. Then a forced laugh. "You are more intelligent than I had guessed, Princess. Well, if you must have it, yes, I would. And life is short. Things happen. Your father met with an unfortunate hunting accident, if you remember. The King's health is poor. Perhaps Prince Kayteth will also meet with bad luck."

"People will suspect."

"I doubt it. Did anyone query the accident that took your parents?"

"You mean . . . ?" She put out a hand to the cold cave wall. "It was murder . . . *you* killed them?"

"You misjudge me, Princess. I would never stoop to anything so crude."

"But you said . . . and the young man . . . "

"I am at heart a statesman. Such people do not dirty their hands with such matters. They are *arranged*."

You slime, she thought. She stood up straight, taking her hand away from the wall. "Then I suppose you will have to *arrange* to have me killed, too, since I am next in succession."

"It *is* a problem." His voice was as unemotional as if he were discussing a theorem in geometry. "If Queen Sankath should become a nuisance, and, with such a woman, one must not discount the possibility, then if you were dead the throne would be . . . well, open to all comers."

"And poor Eskoril might be squeezed right out?"

"After all my work. But it is a possibility. There are those at the palace who do not trust me." He shrugged, his hands spread, the kroklyn driver's gesture. "So, taking the bite with the stride, as Shad would say, it may be better if I allow you to live."

"How kind of you!"

"But on the other hand, I have been telling you rather more

132

than I intended. I wonder why? Are you to be trusted? I think not. Of course, you are still a minor. It would be a simple matter to have you transferred to the Castle of Gander in Komilant to finish your education – a rather slow education."

"You would imprison me?"

"In the lap of luxury, my dear Princess."

"I think I would rather die!"

"No, that would not be allowed. You are my insurance, my dear. If Queen Sankath should become a nuisance then I will marry you and through you inherit the twin thrones. But enough of this talk. We are wasting time. You will show me the way to the secret pool *now*." His voice was icy. Its tone chilled her more than the clammy cave. Oh, if only Jodril were here. . . .

"Very well." She kept her voice steady. "You had better let me carry the torch. It is a pity that you didn't think to bring two."

"I will be the torchbearer, Princess." The edge in his voice told her of his fear.

"Then you will have to lead the way, because without the light I certainly cannot."

They stared at each other, her will against his. It was his that gave. He handed her the torch. She took it without acknowledgment and turned briskly to follow the route she had traveled earlier that day.

Don't let me forget the way, she prayed. He is close to the edge, and if he should think I am playing games with him, he will surely snap.

"Come." She kept her voice steady and at once set out, not looking to see if he was following. The path twisted and turned, branched and came together. Behind her she could hear his panting breath, the occasional scrape of his sandal against a stone. They came to the pit. With the torch in one hand she scrambled quickly down the rope ladder.

"Wait." There was panic in his voice. "Shine the light on the ladder."

When she did so she saw his face, pale and slicked over with oily sweat. His lips were drawn back in a grimace so that she could see his teeth. Like a cornered animal, she thought. She held the torch very steady and walked more slowly down the narrow passage that sloped toward the hot stream.

The smells of the earth spirits moving in the depths were very powerful now, and there were strange rumblings and sighings as if, far below, they were talking softly to each other.

They came to another fork in the passage. Antia stopped, the light flickering uncertainly from left to right.

"What is it? Why have you stopped?"

"I have to think. I can't remember . . . "

"If it's a trick . . . " His hand came up threateningly.

She looked at him coldly, not allowing her eyes to leave his, the way one might calm a frightened horse. "If it were a trick I could have led you astray a hundred times. I could have left you at the top of that ladder."

Then she turned her back on him, her heart thumping, and left him standing with his hand still raised against her. She knelt and examined the floor. It was no help, dry stone with no possibility of footprints. "I'm not sure. I think this is the right way."

She set off more cautiously than before. Eskoril crowded so closely that when she slowed down to check the way, his robes brushed against her. "Give me room," she said between her teeth, and he fell back. But within a minute he was back, crowding close to the light.

There was a turn she did not remember. "I'm wrong. I'm sure I'm wrong." As she stopped her foot kicked a stone. In the same instant Eskoril bumped into her from behind. She fell back against him, clutching the wall of the passage with her free hand. The torch shone down on darkness. The stone she had kicked fell. After a long time they heard a small splash.

Together, bound by their common fear, they fled back to the junction. Once they were on the right path, Antia's legs suddenly gave way under her and she slid onto the floor, her breath coming in shuddering gulps. Her fear seemed to encourage Eskoril. It was as if they were in all things the opposite of each other. When she was strong he was weak. When she faltered . . . She forced herself to her feet again.

"No more mistakes." His voice was bullying again.

"I hope not." She managed a laugh. "Are you ready, Eskoril? Because I must warn you that the worst is yet ahead. Are you ready?"

"Yes. Yes. Go on."

When they came to the rock bridge she stopped and played the torch around, ostensibly to show herself the way, but in fact to make sure that Eskoril fully understood the danger. The powerful light made the crossing seem even more terrifying than had Sandwriter's torches. The narrow neck of rock gleamed against a chasm that was inky black in contrast. She played the light downward, but could see no bottom. She stood to one side to make sure that Eskoril saw.

"I will go first and hold the torch steady for you to cross," she said briskly. "Do not attempt to cross with me. If you crowd me as you did at that last place we will both surely lose our lives."

She turned and walked steadily across the frightful chasm. Suppose my ankle should turn on a pebble? Suppose . . . ? She pushed these demon thoughts out of her mind and concentrated on an image of a flat wide field with a line of flowers down the middle. When it was steady in her mind she walked lightly across the imaginary flowers to the other side.

Once she was a safe distance from the edge she turned and played the light along the neck of the rock, being careful to

135

keep the beam low so that it would not shine in Eskoril's eyes. Even though he was a three times murderer she didn't have the right . . .

He hesitated.

"Come on. It's not really difficult. It just looks frightful."

"I cannot. Come back. There must be another way . . . "

"I know of none. This is the way I was shown."

Perhaps I should turn off the flashlight and crawl away? I might save Roshan that way.

But could she leave Eskoril to die? No, not deliberately, like that. I can't.

She did not know if it was because of all he had been to her when she was growing up in Kamalant, or if she would have felt the same if he had been a stranger, but she found herself talking to him softly, encouragingly.

"It is not so bad. Just one foot at a time. Do not look at the sides, Eskoril. Imagine there is a line down the middle and that is where you are walking. That is the way . . . oh, look out!"

For he had looked down, swayed and fallen to his knees. His eyes were shut. It was on hands and knees that he crawled the rest of the way across.

When he got to his feet there was silence. Antia knew that she was in greater danger than she had ever been in her life before.

"Why are you waiting? What's the matter with you?" he said gruffly, and she turned thankfully and continued along the passage.

Then there came the smell of cool air and the sweetness of living water. She held the torch above her head and diamonds and sapphires seemed to flash from the vaulted ceiling. She played the light on pinnacles and pillars, on bosses and flowing stone draperies. It was even more beautiful in the clear white light of Eskoril's torch than it had been before.

Antia's knees gave way and she collapsed exhausted onto a

smooth rock above the pool. Here, in the quiet heart of Roshan, fear fell away from her. She felt that she could rest here forever. If her plan succeeded she might well have to.

Eskoril snatched the torch from her hand and ran to and fro, exclaiming at each jewel flash, reaching out and then falling back in disappointment when his hand touched, not precious stone, but only rock.

"Is this the place?"

"This is the heart of Roshan. Now I hope you're satisfied." She made her voice sound bitter.

"Then this . . . " He walked slowly forward to the dark pool that Sandwriter had called the navel of Roshan. He bent and touched the surface, sniffed and then licked his fingers. "But . . . this is water. Only water!"

"Of course. This is the heart of Roshan. What else were you seeking? Why, water is life. Water is the beginning of everything."

In three strides he had reached her. She tried not to shrink away. "There is nothing else? This is the secret of Roshan?" She could hear in his voice the despair of a man who has sacrificed everything, including his honor and the lives of others, for a meaningless dream.

"This is the place," she agreed, and tranquilly smoothed her white robe over her knees.

He stood as still as if he had been turned into one of the stone pillars. She dared not move. Please don't make me play my last card. . . .

He grabbed her wrist and twisted it so hard that she screamed. His eyes glared into hers. She could see his unshaven cheeks and smell his sour breath. His eyes were as flat and as pitiless as a snake's. In them she could see all that he had done and would do on the path to his dream.

"This is the pool?"

"I told you . . . " She was close to fainting. She bit the inside of her lip until she could taste blood.

"Then what is that on your robe?"

It was totally unexpected. She looked down. There, dramatically contrasted against her white robe, were the smears of black where, all those hours ago, she had wiped the stickiness of the dark pool off her fingers.

She swallowed and tried to smile. "Mud, I expect. What has that to do with. . . ?"

He grabbed her robe, felt the marks, and sniffed them like a dog. "Liar, liar, liar!" His voice rose to a scream. "It does exist, and you have seen it. Show me now or I'll kill you." His hands encircled her throat. She could feel the iron in his fingers.

"There was a place we passed on the way out. The water was sticky with mud." The steadiness of her voice amazed her. "It's of no importance. *This* is the heart of Roshan."

His hands fell from her throat and he began to laugh. He went on laughing, as if he couldn't stop. A crazy laugh that echoed off the walls and pillars of the cave. Madness all around her. Antia shuddered.

Finally he gasped and stopped. "I believe you're telling the truth, after all. You're as simple as the Roshanites, dear Princess. Worshiping water when you might have the power of methli." He pulled her roughly to her feet. "Come. Show me the way. And no trickery this time."

"Have I tricked you yet? I brought you to the heart of Roshan and I only lost my way once. You should be proud of your pupil, Eskoril."

"Take me to the black pool, to the methli."

She turned away from him and picked up the beaten metal cup that stood on a natural shelf beside the water. She dipped and drank deeply, rejoicing in its sweetness. She refilled the cup and offered it to Eskoril. He swore and pushed it out of her hand. "Which is the way? Show me at once."

138

"Behind a pillar close to the wall there is a narrow cleft. And beyond it . . ." She walked toward the wall, trying to remember. She found the right opening at the second try. A passage led steeply downward. Powerful vapors stung her nostrils and eyes. The air grew hot and stuffy.

Behind her, Eskoril urged her forward. His greed was so evident that it was almost as if there were a third person in the narrow passage with them. Antia imagined what it might look like, heavy-footed, sprawling like a toad, with hot mad eyes. . . .

"There . . . " She shone the torchlight around the cave. Its white beam was swallowed in the inkiness of the pool. Eskoril snatched the torch again and ran forward. He knelt by the pool. He sniffed and touched the surface. He rubbed his hands together, smearing them with the black stickiness. And he laughed. She shivered at the sound which was no longer quite human. Then he stood and turned to her, his mouth twisted in a grin, his eyes glittering. "I must be on my way before dark. You spoke of another way out of here?"

Her heart leaped. He had fallen into her trap. "No, there's no way except . . ."

"Don't play games with me, Princess, or I may forget my insurance and strangle you now and throw you into the pool. I have not forgotten that you told me that you passed this pool on your way *through* the caves. Through. A way in. A way out. Now you are going to tell me, or do I have to make you?"

She backed away and gave a reluctant laugh. "You could always beat me at castles, Eskoril. It is over there." She pointed to the far wall. "It is a steep climb, but quicker than the other," she lied.

He strode past the pool to the far wall. "This opening . . . ?"

"That is the only one I know of. Eskoril, you have the light. Wait for me."

"No, madam. This time *you* will wait. I have to reach

Monar and set sail before you give the warning. The kroklyn will take me, and a fast ship waits for me in the harbor. Once at sea I will be safe. You can say what you will."

"You're going to leave me *here*, in the dark?" Her scream was not all acting.

He laughed mockingly. "You've always been in the dark, you stupid girl. All your fine airs, all the madams and highnesses, just because chance made you the daughter of a prince and me the son of a nobody. Without that accident of birth, you'd be nothing more than a stupid, spoiled child. Think about *that* as you wait."

"I'll die. You'll have lost your insurance then."

"You won't die. Your puppy, Jodril, is doubtless panting on your trail this moment. If you don't find your own way out, he'll reach you by morning. So, Princess, until we meet again, good-bye." He kissed her hand mockingly and then slipped into the passage, leaving the cave in darkness.

At once, while she still had her sense of direction, she felt her way back along the cave wall to the passage through which they had just come. When Eskoril found that she had led him into a dead end she did not want to be close to his anger. If I can only reach the big cave before he returns, she thought, there are a hundred places where I can hide until Jodril comes.

The journey downward to the black pool had seemed to consist of a single twisting passage. But on the way up she had not gone far before her outstretched hands encountered a division in the path. Which way was right? She remembered the other traps they had encountered and shuddered. Without a light it would be madness to go on.

What am I going to do? I daren't go on. I can't go back and face *him*. It was such a neat plan. So simple . . . What am I going to do?

To go back was the only possibility. With a sob of despair she felt her way down the steep path to the cave. Once inside

140

she moved cautiously around to her right. She dared not leave the wall of the cave for an instant. It was her only reality. Out of touch with it she would be lost in the inky blackness. She could stumble right into the pool.

At the thought of the thick sticky blackness covering her mouth, seeping into nose and ears and eyes, she shuddered. She clutched the wall, frozen with fear.

She forced herself to move, to crawl around the wall toward the opening through which Eskoril had gone. The wall seemed to stretch on forever. The cave had grown to the size of a cathedral. She would *never* get there.

Then in the profound silence she heard the sound of a tiny pebble rolling. Eskoril was on his way back, angry at her trick, ready to kill. He had the light and there was nowhere for her to hide.

# 10

Antia flattened herself against the wall of the cave, only wishing it would open up and swallow her. She held her breath and listened. Nothing. Had she imagined the sound?

Then the solid blackness of the cave was broken by the faintest light, a rosy glow coming from her right, farther away than she had expected. Now was her chance, while she could see. She darted across the cave and pressed herself against the wall close to the opening.

She was on the left side. If Eskoril was holding the torch in his left hand she might be able to snatch it from him before he was aware that she was there. Or if that was not possible she might be able to slip into the cleft behind him while he was still searching for her in the cave. He would think that she had managed to get out the other way. Maybe . . .

She bent down and felt around until her hand encountered a stone the size of her palm. It wasn't much of a weapon, but it would have to do. Then she waited. Her heart pounded. How quiet he was!

The glow became stronger. A light fell on the cave floor, a perceptible light. It became dazzling. She hadn't thought of that. She couldn't see for light. But she could still feel, and

142

when the loose sleeve of his robe brushed her arm she reached out her hand . . .

And screamed as it was caught in a grip of iron. She brought up her other hand, the one that held the stone. The stone clattered to the ground and she gasped. For the robed figure was not holding a Kamalant torch but a bale of wood that flickered orange-red and smoked most vilely.

"Sandwriter? Oh, is it really you?" She clung to the frail figure. "Oh, oh."

"Hush, child, it's all right. There is nothing to fear."

"But there *is*. Eskoril is in those passages somewhere. Didn't you see him? When he finds there's no way out he'll come back and kill us both. Oh, quickly!"

"Listen, child. *There is no danger.* There *is* a passage out and Eskoril passed me on his way through it. He did not see me, but I saw him. He is gone and there is nothing for you to fear anymore."

"But that's even worse. What have I done? I didn't know there was another way out. I planned for him to get lost in the passages while I went back the other way and got help."

"Without a light? What a brave child you are!"

"What's the use of being brave when one is stupid? Oh dear, I've ruined everything."

"Antia, listen to me. I am the keeper of the secret of Roshan. Do you think I would allow that secret to escape so easily?"

"But . . . " Antia tried to find words to say that even if Sandwriter were a priestess she would be powerless against a man as ruthless as Eskoril.

"Come with me. There is work still to be done." Sandwriter held high her flaming torch and turned back into the crevice with Antia close behind her. Within, the way lay steeply up a slope that turned, at last, into a series of roughly hewn steps. Up, up they went, until Antia's leg muscles were

143

knotted with cramps and she was gasping for breath. Ahead Sandwriter skipped nimbly along.

"Have courage, child. We are almost there." Sandwriter suddenly turned aside and plunged the flaming torch into a mound of sand. Antia cried out, for it seemed that they were now in total darkness. Then she blinked and saw, directly ahead, a thin bar of light. They squeezed to the left through a narrow passage. The light was on their right. Brighter. They turned. The light was dazzlingly bright. A narrow place where they had to stoop. And then . . .

"Take care." Sandwriter's arm was like an iron bar across Antia's chest, preventing any movement.

At first she could see nothing but the dazzle of rosy light on sand. Then, with a sudden swoop of terror, she realized that they had emerged from the mountain onto a narrow rock shelf high above the desert floor. The sun was low to their left, shadows of dunes scalloped across the sand. Directly ahead to the north lay an empty expanse of desert.

No, it was not quite empty. A small dot moved across the vastness. A small dot heading for Monar.

"Eskoril." Sandwriter pointed.

"We have to stop him. Once he gets to his ship . . . "

"He will be stopped. Now, follow me with great care. If you are not accustomed to mountain climbing you may find it a little difficult."

A little difficult! It should have been impossible. Only the joy of being in the open air, of being free, dulled Antia's fear so that she was able to follow Sandwriter obediently, putting her feet exactly where Sandwriter put hers, and her hands on the handholds Sandwriter used.

Their way led along a narrow shelf that at times was no more than a crack. It meandered across the rock face and slowly, agonizingly slowly, approached the desert floor. When her foot finally touched firm ground she looked up at the dizzying way they had come and could not believe that she had actually been up there.

"Antia, you're safe!"

She turned and there was Jodril with his arms out. "Jodril, I'm so glad to see you." In their hug, all their past differences were forgotten.

"But why did you go off without telling me? You must have known that I'd be frantic. What happened?"

So she had to explain from the beginning. When she had finished, he apologized. "If I had been looking after you instead of sulking, Eskoril couldn't have pulled off that trick. I'm sorry. But you are all right?"

"I'm fine, but Eskoril knows all about the dark pool – methli, he called it. Now he'll get his ship back to Kamalant. He and my aunt are planning to get rid of Uncle Rangor. Then she'll marry Uncle Kayteth and take over Roshan and steal the . . . the methli. And Eskoril threatened to keep me in prison for ever, in case he wants to marry me later and get the throne that way instead of through the Queen. Oh, Jodril, he's so horrible."

He hugged her again. "Crying won't do any good. You're well off without him if you ask me."

"I know. But . . . "

"Come on, Sandwriter wants us to go."

"Thank goodness you brought a kroklyn with you, Jodril. I don't think I could walk another step."

The three of them crowded into the double saddle of the kroklyn. Then, at a word from Sandwriter, it scrambled to its feet and strode off.

"But we're heading in the wrong direction! Eskoril's going north."

"We'd never catch him. Don't worry, Antia. I'm sure Sandwriter has a plan."

Guided by the gnarled hands of the old woman the kroklyn

145

strode around the easterly tip of the mountain. Behind it lay the Great Dune, its scalloped ridge rosy in the evening light. They cantered past its trailing edge and turned westward, until at last Sandwriter halted the beast below the great slope of the central part of the dune. It folded its legs in its usual rocking ungainly way. Before it had reached the ground Sandwriter had slid to the sand. "Wait for me here. I will not be long."

"Let us come with you."

"It is not permitted. Wait in the saddle."

She turned away and they watched the small figure climb rapidly up the slope of the dune to its razorback ridge. She stood with her back to them, so that all they could see of her were her tattered brown garments fluttering in the wind.

Her arms stretched up, and it seemed, just for an instant, that she had touched the sky itself. Antia blinked. Just a mirage, of course. Then Sandwriter's arms fell to her sides and she turned and began to scuttle, crablike, down the side of the dune.

When Jodril reached down and pulled her up into the saddle she leaned against him as if there was no strength left in her body. Her hood fell back and Antia saw eyes filled with pain and sorrow. They closed and her head drooped.

"Oh, she is ill. Hold her tightly, Jodril. I'll guide the kroklyn."

"Take her to the village. To Shudi's house." Jodril's arms closed protectively around the small tattered bundle, and Antia shook the reins, kicked the kroklyn's hairy sides and called to it to make it get up.

As they lumbered towards the shadowy squares that marked the sunken village, Antia glanced over her right shoulder.

"Jodril, look back."

A line of dark crept rapidly across the sky toward them. The thornbushes at their feet shook. The sand stung their ankles. The kroklyn bared its teeth and strode on.

146

Jodril whistled. "It's going to be a beauty!"

They left the kroklyn in the rough shelter at the top of the stairs with the other beasts, and Jodril carried Sandwriter down while Antia ran ahead to warn Shudi of their coming.

The household was in a state of organized chaos. The children were busy running to and fro, carrying buckets of water into the houses. One stood by the well, ready to cover it when the others were through. The men were putting up shutters and getting ready to close the great door at the foot of the stairs. Covers were rigged above the courtyard and the furniture was being hauled into the houses.

"Take this." Shudi thrust her basket of wool and her spindle into Antia's hands. "Jodril, bring her this way." She held open the door and Jodril carried her into the room where Antia had spent so many days.

"What happened?" Shudi's rough hand smoothed the hair from the old woman's forehead.

"She called out the winds. We saw it." Jodril's voice trembled. "She used up all her strength. Shudi, is she going to die?"

"Without a successor? Do not say it, Jodril!" Shudi held her fingers in the bad luck sign and blew on them to blow away the unlucky words. "I think that she will sleep and that when she wakes all will be well. But she is old, too old for such great work as calling out the wind." She tutted and fetched a cloth to bathe the forehead of Sandwriter.

Antia knelt beside her and stared. The eyelids were closed over eyes deeply sunk. The brows were strong and well arched. The nose had the same imperious hawklike curve as Chief Hamrab's, while the mouth, though now surrounded by a hundred tiny wrinkles, was shaped in what must once have been a beautiful curve. Now her face was brown and withered by countless years of wind and sun and sand. But beneath the old skin . . . "Why, she looks just like Jodril's father."

147

"That is not surprising. She was once his aunt," Shudi replied matter-of-factly.

"Really? But . . . what do you mean 'once was'? Isn't she still?"

"To be Sandwriter is to carry a great burden. It is to *be* for all the people and for the land of Roshan rather than to be for oneself. Once, so they say, she was the most beautiful and popular woman in the land. But old Sandwriter reached out and touched her, wrote her name in the sand and called her to come. She left her robes and her friends and her home in Lohat forever. She lived with the Old One, learning all her skills and the secrets of Roshan. Then, when the Old One died, she became Sandwriter."

"And now *she* is the Old One." Antia sat on the bed opposite and stared at the still figure, her chin on her hand. "I wonder if she ever missed being married and having children. And dances and pretty dresses . . . "

"Sssh!" Jodril looked scandalized, but Shudi smiled.

"I expect she did at first. She is still human, as well as being what she is."

They sat in silence. Beyond the closed door and the fastened shutters the wind screamed and the sand blew like fine shot against the walls of the cave house.

"Jodril?"

"Yes."

"She made the storm happen, didn't she? We saw it. But how *could* she?"

"Hush. She is Sandwriter. That is all."

"She knew we had to stop Eskoril. So she called down the wind to do it for her. That was why she was so calm when I thought I had ruined everything. She knew all the time that she could stop him, just by holding up her *arms*. . . . "

"It was more than that. Much more. You can see what it has done to her."

148

They looked at the still small figure. The wind screamed and the sand lashed at the doors and windows. Antia shuddered. "He's out in this nightmare."

"Serve him right."

"One man and a kroklyn. Could he survive?"

"If he were one with the desert he might. But he is its enemy. He sees everything and everyone that way, doesn't he? To be used or thrown aside."

"Jodril, don't!"

"Are you still romantic about him, after everything. . . ?"

"He was once my most dear and special friend, when I had nobody else but Nan. He . . . "

"He would have killed you like *that!*" He clicked his fingers.

"I wonder if he would have, really. . . ." But she remembered the flat, hard look in his eyes and the way he seemed to have enjoyed twisting her arm behind her back till she screamed. She sighed. "Perhaps he would. But that can't change the past and how I felt about him then. Oh, Jodril, why is life such a muddle?"

"It's all right. It'll work out for the best, you'll see. Sandwriter will look after everything."

"If she lives."

"Hush."

After a while Shudi brought them water to drink, flat and warm. "*He* had none," Antia remembered.

"No what?"

"No water. I offered him a drink from the pool, but he threw it away."

They sat in silence. After a time Antia lifted her head. "Jodril, listen!"

"I hear nothing."

"Neither do I. Is the storm over? Do you think . . . ?" She ran into the front room and began to talk to Atmon and the others.

Jodril followed, to find her persuading them to open the

149

door. It opened inward, spilling a mound of sand onto the floor.

"Could we go? Please." Antia was holding Atmon by the arm. He was shaking his head, but like a man who could be convinced to change his mind. "Jodril, please ask him. See if he'll go with us to find Eskoril."

"What's the haste? You don't expect to find him alive, do you?"

"He might be. We survived the other storm with no trouble."

"That was like a summer breeze. Antia, we could hear the wind and sand, when we were safely underground. Imagine what it must have been like on the surface."

"I know. I am. That is why I must go." Her face was white. He shook his head, not convinced.

"Well, suppose you're wrong. Suppose he's alive and still on his way to Monar? If he reaches it ..."

Jodril bit his lip. "What do you think, Atmon? Could we make it now or must we wait until tomorrow?"

Atmon rubbed his chin. "Well, young Chief, I do have two kroklyns who are wicked enough to go through hell and out the other side. Maybe, with them ..."

"Very well. You and me alone. I think. Better not to risk any others of your family."

Atmon nodded and at once became businesslike, packing food, a water bag, a length of rope.

"And what about *me*?" Antia's voice went up.

"You? Really, Antia, you've persuaded us to go. But to take you along ..."

"It's not a question of you *taking* me. I'm going. If I can't ride with you and Atmon, I'll ride alone. I'll go on foot if I must."

Jodril took her hands. "Won't you trust us to look for him properly. I swear we will."

She blinked back tears at the kindness in his voice. "I must go, Jodril. I'm the only one he knows. The only one who loved him."

"After everything he did?"

"That doesn't change the past. I must go, Jodril."

Jodril looked at Atmon, his eyebrows raised. Atmon shrugged, arms out, mouth turned down.

"All right. We'll ride together. After all, she'll be an extra pair of eyes, Atmon."

They tied their robes tightly about their ankles and fastened the loose end of their headcoverings closely about their faces, leaving only a small slit to breathe and see through. We look like three ghosts, thought Antia, wrapped in our burial shrouds. She shivered and quickly blew away the bad luck thought, just as if she were a Roshanite.

They staggered up the sand-strewn stairs, the wind an enemy all the way. They had to shovel mounds of sand away from the kroklyns' shelter before they could force open the door. Inside it was steamily hot. The kroklyns turned their snakelike heads and bared their greenish teeth. Atmon twisted the ear of one beast until it scrambled reluctantly to its feet. Then the second.

Once in the saddle it was possible to see, and the wind ran low, whipping up only the heavier sand around the hairy legs of the kroklyns. It made smoking swirling patterns along the surface of the ground. Will we ever find him in this? Antia wondered in dismay.

They headed north in an early dusk, the sky a dirty brown, the sun a dull blur in the west. It was close to the horizon. They did not have much time left. The kroklyns moved slowly through the fluid mass of wind-borne sand, putting each foot down with maddening care. The wind drove at Antia's body, and she could feel sand against her teeth in spite of her swathes of white cloth. She panicked, suddenly afraid to breathe or

151

swallow. She had a nightmare vision of being filled with sand, filled with Roshan.

Once, long ago, she had had a doll. It was when Father and Mother were alive – before the accident that wasn't an accident. She had cut the doll's body – was it by mistake or in a fit of temper? She couldn't remember. But as if it had just happened, she could remember the stuffing dribbling out and the doll getting emptier and emptier. She had tried to hold the edges together, but it was no good. The sand had all dribbled out until her doll was as flat as desert bread, with just her head intact. How odd it was to think about that doll now, clinging to the saddle, her head against Jodril's shoulder.

Atmon shouted across to Jodril, and the two kroklyns were driven close to each other so that the men could talk above the wind.

"Not much farther, Atmon thinks." Jodril shouted over his shoulder to Antia. "We're going to head to the left for two hundred paces while Atmon searches to the right. Then we'll turn, come back to meet each other, go forward fifty paces and turn to each side again. You count the kroklyn paces and I'll look out. My eyes are desert trained."

The two kroklyns parted, each heading in a direction at right angles to the path that they guessed Eskoril had taken. They would comb four hundred paces this way. Not a very wide margin of error. If he had strayed . . . She began to count.

". . . one hundred and ninety-nine. Two hundred." She thumped Jodril's back and he turned the kroklyn forward and then back. Two hundred paces later she saw the shadowy figure of Atmon, his beast a sand-matted hulk in the lessening wind. Together they paced forward and again turned to left and right.

As she counted, Antia peered through the slit in her head-covering. Suppose Jodril were to miss him? Suppose they were to ride right by and leave him to die? A flutter caught her eye and she yelled to Jodril.

"Thornbush," he shouted back. "Keep counting."

"I am. Ninety-one, ninety-two . . . two hundred." They turned and again met Atmon at precisely the count of two hundred. How many generations had it taken to give to Jodril and Atmon this kind of knowledge?

After the fifth pass, the two men met to confer. "Atmon thinks it's hopeless and we should stop now. If Eskoril strayed off the beaten track to Monar he could be anywhere."

"You want to go back *now*?"

"It's nearly dark."

"Not yet, please. I know he's out there. And the wind has almost dropped. We're able to see farther every minute."

"But once night falls we'll see nothing at all. If the sky doesn't clear quickly it will be hard to find our way back without the stars."

"Just one more time." She kicked the shaggy sides of the kroklyn. Jodril grabbed the reins as the beast moved forward.

"The very last try, then. Once more, Atmon." The ghost figure on the other kroklyn raised a silent hand in acknowledgment. Antia counted fifty paces forward. They turned to the left.

"One, two, three . . . " Her eyes strained. If only she had the eagle vision of the Roshanites. It was getting much darker. " . . . one hundred and ninety-nine, two hundred," she muttered under her breath. She raised her hand to thump Jodril's back. Her hand seemed to stop by itself. She went on counting quietly.

"Aren't we nearly there?" Jodril yelled.

"Almost."

She felt his body stiffen and she thought he had guessed her lie and was mad at her. I don't care, she thought. It felt right.

But he was leaning forward, peering through the gloom.

He turned the kroklyn hard right and jogged forward. At first Antia couldn't see it at all. Then there was just a piece of cloth tugged by the persistent wind. Flapping, but not being blown away.

Before Jodril could force the kroklyn to its knees, Antia had flung herself from the saddle and was sliding down its shaggy side. She ran forward, stumbling through the loose wind-blown sand.

"Antia, don't."

She paid no heed. She could see his shoulders clearly now. They were bowed so that his head was hidden. She tugged at him. How heavy he was! She pulled harder and he rolled heavily over onto his back. The eyes stared at nothing and the mouth was full of sand.

She screamed then, and Jodril's arms were around her, lifting her up, pulling her away. Then their kroklyn lifted its head, snorted and whinnied shrilly. There was a faint answering whinny. Out of the gloom trotted Eskoril's mount. Its head hung low and it stood quietly beside them, its reins dragging.

"Antia, are you all right now? Can you hold its head?"

"Yes. Yes, of course." She realized at once what he had to do. She grasped the reins of Eskoril's mount and pulled on them. The kroklyn collapsed to its knees and breathed warm wet puffs of breath into her ear. She stared steadfastly into the distance until her eyes watered. Behind her, she heard Jodril grunt. Then the kroklyn twitched as it took the sudden load in its saddle. She held the reins tightly and talked soothingly to it.

"Just a minute more. I'm going to tie him to the saddle. Then the reins to the back of our saddle. It'll follow behind well enough. It looks completely broken. He must have ridden it like a fiend."

"He was trying to outride the wind." Her voice broke. "Poor Eskoril." She tried to give Jodril the reins, but she had

154

been holding them so tightly that he had to unwrap her fingers, one by one. After he had fastened the reins to their saddle, he helped her up and kicked their kroklyn into motion.

They rode back in silence. "Two hundred and forty-three," said Jodril unexpectedly, as they saw Atmon, waiting patiently for them. "I *knew* you had gone farther than two hundred."

The wind had dropped to a gentle breeze, and above them the sky slowly cleared. They walked the kroklyns back to the village, Atmon leading the way by the stars, which reluctantly showed through gaps in the cloud-tattered sky.

They were met by Shudi's oldest daughter. "Sandwriter opened her eyes, just a short time ago. She is well."

"I must tell her that we found Eskoril, that it's all right. Antia, will you come with me?"

"No, I don't want to see her. No . . . " She drew back.

"But . . . "

"Leave it." Shudi pushed Jodril through into the inner room. Then she made Antia sit with the rest of the family in the outer room. She gave her a drink of water and gently wiped the sand and sweat from her face. Then she told her daughter to unplait Antia's long black hair and brush the sand from it.

As the brush softly stroked down her head Antia found herself thinking of Nan, dear fat comfortable Nan, who had nothing to do with prophecy or wind calling or the death of men. She burst into tears.

"Oh, I'm sorry. Oh, Mam, did I pull the lady's hair?"

"No, no," Shudi soothed. "Go on brushing. Her tears must come and it is good that they come now."

When Antia had finished crying, Shudi washed her face again. "Do you want to talk about it, my dear?"

"He looked so awful, not like Eskoril at all. Yet like the man in the cave. Perhaps the Eskoril I thought I knew never existed. Perhaps the awfulness really was him." She sighed and a last sob escaped in a hiccup.

Shudi stroked her hair. "I expect many years ago there was a little boy who really was Eskoril. Then he grew up and became envious and greedy and he learned to play clever games. And he forgot all about the little boy who was good and loved his mother."

"It's so sad." Antia blew her nose.

"Waste is sad. That is the saddest thing about evil, that it wastes what could have been good."

Antia nodded. Then her head went on nodding by itself and felt suddenly so heavy that she felt it might roll off. When she opened her eyes it was morning and she was lying on one of the bed shelves in the front room of Shudi's house.

She sat up, much more cheerful after a night's sleep. But when Jodril came in from the back room to say that Sand-writer wanted to see her, she drew back. "I don't want to. Must I, Jodril?"

"She is asking for you specially. And she *is* Sandwriter."

"So . . . ?" Antia stuck her chin up.

"She is Roshan. Antia, what's the matter with you?"

"You know."

"Oh. Yes." He ran his hands through his hair until it stood up and made him look about ten years old. She suddenly wanted to smooth it down for him. She clutched her hands together. "Eskoril would have killed you," Jodril went on.

"I know that."

"He was a terrible man."

"I know that, too. But so much power in one old woman. It's scary. It doesn't feel right."

"Atmon told me this morning that the kroklyn he rode will have to be destroyed. It'll never be able to work again."

"What has that to do with it?"

"Eskoril would never have reached Monar anyway. The

156

kroklyn would have dropped dead under him long before he got there."

"You're telling me that Sandwriter didn't really kill Eskoril?"

"He killed himself, can't you see? All the decisions he ever made finally came to a point when he gave Sandwriter no other choice but to call up the wind. Do you think she likes that kind of power? Do you think she's glad?"

"All right. All right. Don't go on so. If it's that important I'll talk to her."

The inner room was cool and dark, smelling of rock and tallow lamps. Sandwriter was sitting cross-legged on one of the bed shelves. Her hands were folded in her lap and her eyes were downcast. She looked up when Antia came in and motioned for her to sit.

"Is your heart more tranquil today, child?"

"Yes. I suppose it is. But I can't help seeing him, the way he was, you know. His mouth full of sand."

"Roshan accepted him in its own way, though he could never accept Roshan. Now his body will become part of the desert, part of the sand and the wind."

"I offered him water in the sacred cave. He wouldn't take it. He must have been so thirsty at the end."

"His mouth was already full of sand. Of ignorance and greed."

Antia sighed. There seemed to be nothing to say.

"What will you do now, Princess?" The tone was different. She looked up.

Matters of state, Eskoril had called them. She felt very old. "I have to go back to Kamalant and tell my uncle what has been going on behind his back. It will not be easy. In his own way I think he loves my aunt. But I must warn him."

"Yes. There may be other Eskorils at court. A weak king makes for bad servants."

"He *is* weak, but he was always kind."

"As you are compassionate. You will make a good queen when the time comes. It will be soon, I believe."

"But I know nothing at all. I will be hopeless."

"You will do it and you will learn. Will you return to Roshan?"

"I hope so. I wasn't sure I wanted to after last night. But now I know I do." She thought of the wide sky above the wide desert. Of how it emptied one of pride and ambition and envy, so that all that was left was the miracle of being human. "I do hope I can come back."

"You will leave today?"

"Yes. I mustn't delay."

The old woman's eyes closed. It was as if she had gone away somewhere outside her body. Then her eyes opened and she looked at Antia. "Of course. That is evident." She seemed to be speaking, not to Antia, but to some other person. She stood up and took Antia's hands. "Before you leave I would like you and Jodril to come with me to the dune."

Shortly before noon the three of them stood together on the sharp scalloped crest of the Great Dune, the same place where Sandwriter had stood to call down the wind. It blew now, as it always did, strongly enough to smoke the loose grains of sand off the upmost ridge, so that it was continually erased and replaced.

"You wrote your name in the sand once before, child, not knowing what you did. In doing so you gave yourself to Roshan, though you were a stranger then, a Kamalantan. Would you write it again now, knowing what it means?"

Antia stood and looked at the red cliff rearing out of the sand, hiding the two secrets of Roshan. At the stretch of desert that reached to the limit of her vision in every other direction. She looked up at the empty sky where two tiny specks circled lazily in a thermal. She felt as small as a grain of sand and as great as the whole world of Rokam. A grain of sand. Or a planet. Like a pendulum. First one. Then the other. The two . . .

She looked at Sandwriter, saw the smile on the old woman's lips. "I do not understand, but, yes, I will write my name." She knelt to write her full royal title in the sand of Roshan.

"You, Jodril, son of Hamrab? Will you write your name with Antia's?"

Jodril started and blushed. "It is your will, Sandwriter?"

"Only if it is yours."

"Is it possible? Could it be?"

"I see two houses united in peace. I see a child coming to me from that union. Do not make me wait too long for that child. I have much to teach and I am growing old."

Smiling, Jodril knelt beside Antia to write his name. They knelt and watched the wind blur the grains of sand, blowing them away to mingle together and become part of the land of Roshan forever.